Prayers and Promises

Timeless Gospel stories

Prayers and Promises

Frances Bevan

Christian Focus Publications

This edition
Copyright © 2005 Christian Focus Publications
ISBN 1-84550-038-5

Published by
Christian Focus Publications,
Geanies House, Fearn, Tain, Ross-shire,
IV20 1TW, Scotland, United Kingdom.

Originally published as Seven True Stories

www.christianfocus.com
email: info@christianfocus.com

Cover design by Catherine Mackenzie

Printed and bound by Nørhaven Paperback A/S,
Viborg, Denmark

Contents

Part One

Part Two

Preface

These true stories are written down just as they have been told to children on Sunday afternoons. God is always working in his own blessed way in the hearts of sinners, drawing them to Christ. He is always working for the instruction and encouragement and joy of his people. He uses ways and means, strange and insignificant perhaps in our eyes, to bring us to know him better, and trust him more completely. He orders the events of our lives so that we may learn something more of his love for us, those he has redeemed for himself, and whom he is preparing for eternal fellowship with him.

The more we observe these things, the more we discover that the Lord Jesus Christ is dear to our hearts.

Some of these stories show us the wonderful and unexpected ways by which sinners learn of the Lord Jesus.

May you be encouraged by these stories to tell others to trust in the Lord Jesus Christ.

Part One

Blankets and a Prayer

There was once a poor woman who lived with her husband and ten children in a mews in the west end of London. Those of you who have never seen London, must remember that the stables belonging to London houses were all built together, somewhere behind or near the houses to which they belonged, and all these stables joined together are called mews. So that a mews was like a little town of stables and coach-houses, with rooms above, where the coachmen and other stablemen lived, with their wives and children.

The families living in the mews were hardly ever visited or looked after by their rich neighbours, and the children ran about and played in front of the stables from morning to night, never going to school, and learned only to be rude and wicked.

The poor woman of whom I am telling you, wished to bring her children up well. That means that she wished them to be well-behaved and clean, and she did her best to make them so. But it never crossed her mind that they had souls to be saved, or even that she herself had a soul. If she knew that there is a God, she thought no more about him than of some heathen idol whose name we might have heard.

No wonder that poor Mrs Clare was a very unhappy woman. She was seldom well, and she had hard work to look after the children, and to find means to feed and clothe them. Her husband was only a helper in a gentleman's stables, and his wages were small.

And at last one day there came a sad piece of news to Mrs Clare. The gentleman told her husband that he was going away immediately to America, for a long time, and that he should want him no more, for he would sell his carriage, horses and furniture. But he said that Clare might stay on in his rooms in the mews till another job arose or another gentleman bought the house and stables, whichever came first. But some of the furniture in the family's rooms, which belonged to the master, would be taken away at once, to be sold with the furniture of the house.

Mr Clare did not much mind losing these few bits of furniture, for the rest, which was his own, was enough for the time at least. But Mrs Clare thought at once of a part of the Master's property, which she would be very unwilling to lose. All the blankets belonged to him. And now winter was coming, and her husband would be unemployed and they could never afford to buy new blankets. Mrs Clare's only hope was that, as the blankets were old and thin, the master would not think it worthwhile to take them away. But the very thought that he might was terrible to her.

Mrs Clare was not accustomed to having visitors, and as she sat there, feeling very sad and forlorn, she was startled by the sight of a strange woman who stood at the door, asking if she might come in. This woman was employed in selling Bibles. But it was of no use to offer one to Mrs Clare. In the first place she had no money; in the second place she could not read and, alas, in the third place she had never had any desire to know anything of the word of God. So she refused the Bible very civilly.

'You look unhappy,' said the Bible-woman.

'I may well be unhappy,' said Mrs Clare, 'for I don't know how we are all to live now my husband has lost his job, and I'm always ill, and I have such a number of small children,' and poor Mrs Clare began to cry.

'Do you ever pray about it?' asked the Bible-woman.

'Pray!' said Mrs Clare, opening her eyes very wide. 'No, I never prayed in my life. It's the parsons that pray.'

'But everyone may pray,' said the Bible-woman. 'Do you really mean to say you never knelt down on your knees to pray to God?'

'Well, I do remember I knelt down once,' said Mrs Clare, after thinking a moment.

'I knelt down in the church the day I was married; but it was the parson that prayed.'

'Have you never been to church since?'

'No, neither before nor since.'

'Nor to chapel, nor to a meeting?'

'No I don't go to anything of the sort. I haven't time for that, like the gentry.'

The Bible-woman seems not to have known where to begin in explaining matters to a woman who was plainly so ignorant as Mrs Clare. So, after thinking in vain how to enlighten her, she only said — 'Praying is just speaking to God, and telling him what we want. So if you have never done it before, I advise you to do it now.' And as there were many more houses to visit, the Bible-woman went on her way, and left Mrs Clare with a new thought in her mind.

'Praying is speaking to God, and telling him what we want. Why I think I could do that. It would be like speaking to a friend. It would be a comfort to tell him. I will tell him about the blankets.'

And then and there Mrs Clare knelt down and told the Lord quite simply about the whole matter, and she said — 'O Lord, do not let the master take away the blankets, for we do want them so much.'

The next morning, quite early, the men came who were sent to take the master's furniture to the sale. Mrs Clare said not a word about the blankets, but she watched them anxiously. She felt sure that the Lord had heard her prayer, and yet her heart misgave her when she saw them take off the bedclothes. One by one they rolled up the six old blankets, and carried them away with the other things.

Mrs Clare now felt that there was a trouble even greater than the loss of all her blankets. It had seemed to her such a beautiful thought that the Lord cared for her, and that she might speak to him and tell him of all her wants. And she had really believed that he heard her, and would be her friend. Yet it now seemed clear as the day that it was of no use to pray to him and she felt all alone in the great wide world in a way she had never felt before. She seemed not only to have lost the blankets, but to have lost the Lord too.

At that moment Mrs Clare was roused from her sad thoughts by a loud, quick knock at the door. She opened it, and to her utter astonishment she saw the very last person in the world she could have expected to see.

This person was her sailor brother. He had gone to China not long before and though Mrs Clare was not learned in geography, she had made a good guess in thinking that China was quite the other side of the world, and she knew Jem was to be there a long time.

'Oh, Jem, I'm so glad to see you,' she said.

'So am I glad to see you, Sukey,' said Jem, 'but it's how d'ye do and goodbye, for I only came ashore in the East India Docks this morning, and I'm off by the next train from Waterloo Station to Portsmouth. But I said, "I shall just have time to go round on the way to see Sukey," and I've brought a whole cab full of blankets in case you want them, and they're down at the door below. So now, Sukey, if you care to have them, we'll go down to the cab and clear out the cargo.'

'Why, Jem, how could you know that was just the very thing I want?' said Sukey. And she ran downstairs after him, and helped him to carry the huge parcel up to her little room, where Jem undid it and pulled out one blanket after another – large, beautiful, thick blankets, such as Sukey had never before beheld.

'Perhaps there will be six of them,' she thought. Yes, there were six and six more besides.

'Why, Jem, how did you come by them? And what made you bring them?'

'It's just this,' said Jem. 'You know there's a war in China, and I and five of my mates were wounded, and wouldn't be any good for weeks to come. So they just put us on board an East Indiaman, and sent us home, and they gave us each a pair of navy blankets, because we should have to be in our hammocks for most of the way home. And they told us when we went on shore we might have the blankets for our own. And when we landed this morning, the first thing we heard was that we were to go on to Portsmouth if we were fit for service. And then my mates said, 'What shall we do with the blankets, for they won't be any good to us on board another ship?' and I said, 'Well, I've got a sister in London, with a lot of small children, and maybe she'd like to have mine, so I'll just take them to her and go on to Waterloo.' Then they said, 'You'd better take the whole lot, for we haven't sisters in London, nor anyone who'd care to have them.' So here they are, and now I must be off.' With these words Jem drove off in his cab, and left Mrs Clare happier than he had any idea of.

It was a fine thing to have twelve beautiful blankets in the place of six old thin ones. But it was a greater thing to know that there is a living God, who not only hears prayers, but who does for us far more than we ask or think.

Mrs Clare now knelt down again to thank the Lord. And when she had thanked him, she said to him, 'O Lord, thou knowest we have another trouble. Thou knowest we want nineteen and sixpence. O Lord, please let us have it in time to pay the baker on Saturday.'

Whilst Mrs Clare had been so unhappy about the blankets she had almost forgotten that the baker had said he could no longer go on letting them have bread without being paid for all the bread that they had had for weeks past.

'So,' he had said, 'on Saturday next I shall leave off letting you have any more bread, and I shall send you a summons, if you don't pay me nineteen and sixpence by twelve o'clock that day. For that's what the bill will come to by Saturday.'

Mrs Clare felt sure the Lord would send her this money. But her husband came home very sad and hopeless, saying he had been everywhere to try to get a job, and could hear of nothing. So it was the next day and the next.

Then came Saturday morning. 'I'll try again,' her husband said; 'and though it's only five o'clock I'll start and see what can be done.'

It seemed strange to go out at five o'clock in the morning, when everyone was in bed, to try to get a job. But the Lord had put this thought into Mr Clare's mind. But he didn't know then that it was God who was guiding him.

In an hour's time he came back. He put a sovereign into Sukey's hand, and said, 'Go and pay the baker.'

Now Sukey had not said a word to him about the baker, not about her prayers. But she was sure that the money would come in time.

'How did you get it?' she asked.

'Just as I went out of the mews,' said her husband, 'I saw a gentleman's carriage upset in the Knightsbridge Road, and I went to help; and when it was all done the gentleman gave me a sovereign. I suppose they were coming home from a party somewhere so it's well I went out so early.'

Sukey went to pay the baker, having thanked the Lord for his goodness. And now she felt that the time was come when it was wrong to keep silence about all that he had done for her. So she told her husband all about it; and when the Bible-women came again a few days after, she told her, too, and she asked if there was no place near where a poor woman like herself could go and hear more about God. 'For now,' she said, 'I want to learn all about him. But I can't go to any grand place, where people go with fine clothes, for I've nothing but my old gown, and I shall have to take the baby with me.'

Then the Bible-woman told her that a room had been opened in a mews close by, where there was preaching every Sunday afternoon – nothing to pay, and all might go in just as they were, and find a comfortable seat, and hear about the Lord Jesus in plain words that they could understand.

So Mrs Clare went there the very next Sunday, and there she heard the wonderful story that was to make her happy all her life long, and for ever afterwards. She heard that God not only cares that men and women and children should have food and clothes and beds, but that he so loves his dear people, even long before they love him, that he sent his own Son from heaven, to take upon himself the punishment of all their sins, of all their ingratitude and forgetfulness of him, and their despising him and esteeming him not.

Now Mrs Clare felt for the first time that she was a guilty sinner. She had lived all her life, till the day the Bible-woman came, without one thought of this good and loving God. And it was indeed blessed news to her that, instead of a punishment for all this sin, there was nothing for her in the heart of God but love and tenderness. So that she might have no punishment he had sent his Son to bear it himself and to pay all the great debt and had given her besides the endless riches of his love to be hers forever.

'I have something better than blankets to thank him for now,' she said to the Bible-woman.

It is always a sure mark that God has poured into our hearts the riches of his love, when we wish to share his joy and happiness with those around. For this wonderful happiness is like a flame of fire, which does not grow less but greater as it spreads from one to another.

Mrs Clare became very anxious that her husband should go with her to the preaching. But no, he always had some excuse, and it was plain that he was displeased at hearing all this new sort of talk. It made him feel very uncomfortable, for his eyes were beginning to be opened to see that he was a guilty sinner also.

17

Mrs Clare, however, went on beseeching him to go to the preaching and at last he said, 'Very well; I'll go next Sunday if only you can get my coat out of the pawnshop, for I can't go without a coat.'

He felt quite sure when he said this that it was a very safe promise, for he knew well Sukey had never so much as a penny to spare when the end of the week came. She had got some work as a charwoman at a gentleman's house, and every Saturday morning the housekeeper paid her ten shillings, but then there was all the bread and everything else to be paid for out of that ten shillings; and there was never a farthing over when that was done.

Mrs Clare knew this too, but she knew also to whom to go for the money she needed to get the coat out of the pawnshop. She went to tell the Lord all about it, and then she said to the Bible-woman, 'You'll see my husband at the preaching next Sunday.'

Sunday came and there was Mr Clare in his best coat, and looking, too, as if he was glad to be there.

'How did you get the coat, Mrs Clare?' asked the Bible-woman afterwards.

'When the housekeeper paid me on Saturday morning,' said Mrs Clare, 'she said, "You must give me change for I have nothing but a sovereign," and I said I had no change, and never had so much at a time, nor was likely to have. Then she said, "You must take the sovereign, then, and remember next Saturday that I've paid you." So then I went to the pawnshop and got the coat, and the Lord will see that I'm none the worse off when next Saturday comes.'

18

After this Mrs Clare was better off, for her husband got some work. He did not tell her that he had also got a Bible from the Bible-woman. He was rather afraid and ashamed lest this should be known, but he went on going to the preaching, and all his spare time he went into the loft where he had hidden the Bible amongst the hay, and he read it for hours.

At last he could keep his secret no longer, and he told his wife that 'a change had come over him,' and that he saw she was right, and that the Lord who had opened his eyes had saved him from his sins.

I can tell you no more about Mrs Clare and her husband. Many years have passed since I last heard of or saw them. It may be that she has had many, many more answers to her prayers; and now that she knows the Lord Jesus, as she did not know him at first, she no doubt understands that all is well when he does not give her exactly the thing she asks for. He showed her when she was ignorant of him that he is the living and true God by giving her just the very thing she asked for. But when we know God and his great love, he is able to treat us as a kind father often treats his children. He will sometimes have to say, 'I know you can trust my love, if I refuse to give you the thing you want, and you may be sure I do so that you may have something better, though you may have to wait for it.' So, if we have believed in the love of God, we can be quite happy and peaceful, leaving all in his hands. 'He that spared not his own Son, but delivered him up for us all, how shall he not with him also freely give us all things?'

The Half-crown

It was a cold winter's afternoon, when the snow was lying in patches on the ground, and more snow seemed just ready to fall. A girl called Effie had, nevertheless, started on a long walk to the nearest town. A narrow, winding lane led to the town, and about half-a-mile before the town was reached, the lane took a sudden turn, and passed in front of a row of wretched cottages. They were not the pretty, old thatched cottages of country villages, but they were like a row of dirty houses from the worst and poorest city, moved just as they were to the side of this country lane. The people who lived in them, too, were not like the country people we see here, with clean smock frocks and sun bonnets, but they were dressed in the grimy, ragged clothes that the poor wear in the back street of slums, with bits of dirty finery here and there stuck on the bonnets of the women and girls. But some had no bonnets and no caps, and their long, rough hair hung about their faces.

As Effie turned the sharp corner at the end of this row of cottages she found herself in a crowd of these people, men, women, and children all huddled together, some laughing and some shouting. To her great relief a policeman, whom she knew, forced his way through the crowd, and said to her,

'I will see you safe past, miss. There's a fight going on, and I shall have to stop it, but I will see you safe through the gate into the field path, first.' The policeman then made a way for Effie to cross the road to the wicket-gate, and as they passed through the crowd she saw the horrible sight of a man and woman fighting furiously. Their sleeves were tucked up and their fists doubled. They were just making a violent rush at one another, when the policeman, who had seen Effie safe on the other side of the gate, seized the man and led him off to the door of his wretched house. He then shut the door upon him, and ordered the crowd to disperse. The woman remained standing in the road. She was quite young, scarcely grown up. She had a coarse, but not altogether ugly face. Her old straw bonnet was torn to tatters, and her rough black hair streamed in the bitter wind.

The policeman came back to Effie and said, 'I hope it has not frightened you.

'No,' replied Effie, 'but it was a dreadful sight.'

'And the most dreadful part of it,' said the policeman, 'is that the man and the girl who were fighting are a father and daughter!'

As the policeman spoke these words a window was thrown open in the top storey of the house, and the father's enraged face appeared there. Shaking his fist, he shouted to the girl below, 'Get you gone! You will never put your foot inside this door again. Be off with you, you wicked, good-for-nothing hussy.'

'If I'm wicked and good for nothing,' replied the girl, in a loud, sullen voice, 'it's your fault for bringing me up as you did.'

The father made no answer. He shut down the window with a bang, and disappeared. The girl stood for a moment looking at the window. Then she turned towards the town, and walked slowly on, dragging her ragged slipshod shoes along through the half-thawed snow. Her gown hung in tatters and she had only an old, thin shawl, in tatters also.

Effie walked on, following this wretched girl, and soon overtook her. 'Where are you going?' she said.

'I don't know,' the girl said. 'I haven't nowhere to go.'

'Where will you sleep tonight?'

'I don't know; I haven't no place to sleep in.'

'Have you no friends or relatives in the town?'

'No, I don't know anyone nearer than St. Albans, and that's ten miles on.'

'Do you think you can get there tonight?'

'No, I couldn't walk so far, and it'll be dark in an hour or two.'

Effie was perplexed. She, too, knew no one in the town to whom she could apply for a shelter for the girl. But she did not think that the Lord Jesus would like her to leave the girl wandering about in the snow without a home. Bad as she was, Effie knew that he cared about the girl. Suddenly Effie remembered that there were five good old ladies, all unmarried sisters, who lived together in the town, and who were very kind to the poor for the love of the Lord Jesus. Effie did not know them, but she determined to go and ask them what was to be done.

'What is your name?' she said to the girl.

'Anne.'

'Very well, Anne, now come with me. Tell me when you last had anything to eat.'

The girl thought for a minute, and said, 'It must have been this time yesterday.'

'You have had nothing today? How hungry you must be! You see that baker's shop. Take this twopence and go in there, and buy some bread and wait there till I come back.'

Anne looked pleased. I am not sure whether she had the manners to say, 'Thank you.'

Effie meanwhile hurried off to the pleasant old brick house of the five old ladies. But, alas! Even on that cold afternoon they were one and all out, and not likely to be home for some time. Effie walked back slowly in the direction of the baker's shop. She knew not what to do next. As she passed the shoemaker's, she noticed in the shop two ladies who were trying on shoes. She knew them only by sight, but she had often heard that they were people who loved the Lord Jesus. She felt sure that for his sake they would help her. So she went into the shop and told them the sad story of Anne, and that she was now eating her bread at the baker's shop down the street.

The kind ladies went immediately with Effie to see what could be done. It was now beginning to get dark. 'You must go home,' they said to Effie,

'for you have a long way to go. Leave the girl to us.
We will take her to a safe lodging, and think what
is the best thing to do with her afterwards. We will
let you know tomorrow, when we have enquired
more about her, what seems to be the right plan.'

Effie thanked them warmly for their kindness
and Anne looked quite softened at finding that
there were really people in the world who cared
what became of her.

The next day the kind ladies sent Effie a note.
They said that the town missionary had been down
to see Anne's father, and had persuaded him to take
her back and to treat her well for a few days; but
he would not allow her to go on living at home,
and it would be a pity if he did wish it, for the
whole family were such low, bad people – the only
hope for Anne would be to take her away and put
her somewhere amongst kind Christian friends who
would care for her, and try to train her into the
ways of a tidy servant girl. As she was, nobody
would take her as a servant, nor would she be fit
to do any of the work required in a decent house.
'There are nice homes in London,' the lady went on
to say, 'where girls are trained and taught, and we
will enquire about them, and let you know when we
have found the right place.'

A few days later the direction was sent to Effie
of a training home, where Anne could be taken in
at once, and kept for some months till she was fit
to be a servant. The payment would be five shillings
a week. Effie at that time had no money, but she
knew there was no time to be lost, and that God

would provide all that was wanted, so she went to the wretched house at the corner of the lane, and asked to see Anne's mother. A tall, gaunt, hard-faced woman, with frizzy hair, made her appearance. Effie told her the plan that had been made for Anne, and asked her if she was willing to let her go to the home.

'I'm willing enough,' replied Mrs. B. 'She's only going to the bad here at home, and I don't know what to do with her.'

'Very well,' said Effie. 'They will have room for her next week, on Thursday, so I will tell them to expect her.'

'It's no use for them to expect her,' replied the woman,' unless I go with her every step of the way; for, as sure as she gets to London, she'll be off tramping about the streets and keeping away from every place where she'd be put to work at anything.'

'You shall take her, then,' said Effie. 'Will you promise me to take her on Thursday, next week?'

'Well, I will if I can,' she replied 'But you see, miss, I haven't a penny for the railway ticket, and I shall want a return ticket too. Half-a-crown that will be altogether, and how am I to get it?'

'I will send you the half-crown,' Effie said even though her last penny had been spent at the baker's shop. She knew no one to whom she would like to go for help. Most of her friends were shocked at her for having anything to do with the people who lived in the disreputable cottages. But I do not think the idea ever came into her mind of asking anyone for half-a-crown. God is always able to provide us with everything that is really needful. So Effie told no one what she wanted.

Day after day passed. Monday evening came; a relation asked Effie to go with her to London the next morning, to spend a few hours there. They were to go by train, and the station was two or three miles off. Effie preferred walking there, and promised to be at the station by the time the carriage arrived with her relation. The snow had now completely thawed, and the roads were in a terrible condition. Effie reflected that her muddy country boots would be an unwelcome sight in the London drawing-rooms; she therefore put on some thin house boots, with high india-rubber galoshes over them. On reaching the station she took off the galoshes, and asked the ticket man if he would kindly take care of them till her return. In the afternoon, when she came back, he returned her the galoshes, and she walked home in them. She was taking them off in her room when something fell out of one of them. It was half-a-crown.

'That is for Anne,' was her first thought.

Her second was, 'The half-crown belongs to the railway company. The ticket man will find his accounts wrong this evening; he must have dropped it into the galosh.'

She remembered that the gardener, who would be just starting to go home, lived near the station. She ran down to him, and gave him the half-crown, desiring him to explain to the ticket man where she had found it. Had Effie known all that she found

26

out later on, namely, that the gardener was both a thief and a drunkard, she would certainly not have trusted him on such an errand. But a power greater than the love of drink directed the gardener's steps that evening. He walked past two public-houses, and delivered his message honestly.

The next morning he brought back the half-crown. 'The ticket man found his accounts all right,' he said, 'and he wished me to say he had no right to the half-crown, and that it would be impossible to find the owner, as no doubt some traveller dropped it who may be far in the north by this time.'

So Effie had no scruples about sending the half-crown to Anne's mother. She was even more sure now that all the money needed — even the five shillings every week to keep Anne in the home — would be given — somehow. She therefore left the whole matter in the hands of him to whom all the silver and gold belongs, on earth and under it.

A few days later she received a letter from the matron of the home. Anne was going on well and happily. But the reason of the matron's writing was to ask whether Effie would allow Anne's board and teaching to be paid for by a kind donation. Some good Christians had been brought to see the home. They had been very much pleased with it, and had said that they would like to pay for a girl. The girls were then all sitting at their work, and one had pointed to Anne, and had said, 'That is the girl we will pay for.'

So now all was settled, and Effie had nothing to do but to thank the Lord for thus providing all that was needed. What became of Anne? This is a sad part of the history. She went on well for a time, and learnt enough to be able to take a place as servant. But she did not remain long in her place, she came back to her old home. Effie then saw her again. She was wonderfully altered. She looked neat and respectable, and her hard, coarse face was softened, and had even a kind and almost sweet expression. A short time after her return, she came to tell Effie that her little sister, who was nine or ten years old, was very ill.

'I believe she's going to die,' said Anne; 'but she is quite happy. She says she wants to die and go to Jesus. It was a little hymn-book that I brought from the home that has made her feel like that. She make me read it and sing to her, and she says Jesus loves her, and has washed all her sins away. It's beautiful to see her, and to hear all she says.'

A day or two later the little girl left her wretched home to go to the Good Shepherd who had come to seek and to save her. But poor Anne gave no proof that she, too, had been saved. She was a very different girl from the rude, wild Anne of former days; but she confessed that she could not feel as her little sister did. She did not feel that she could believe, as her little sister had done, in the love of Jesus to her. Anne did not take God at his word. He said that he laid upon his blessed Son the iniquities of lost sinners, and that by him all that believe are justified from all things.

'Christ died for our sins.' Five little words! Yet to believe them is to be saved. Anne went away soon after, and, I believe, married an ungodly man. It may be that some of the texts and hymns she learnt in the home came back to her later on. Perhaps it may have been for the sake of the little sister that Anne was taken for a time where she could hear of Jesus, and become the owner of the hymn-book which led the little girl to the Saviour. We shall know some day. Meanwhile, let us learn from all that the Lord does how he can and will provide for every real need, and let us go to him in perfect trust to tell him all our wants, even if it be but the need of a half-crown.

The Man that Vanished

Effie was asked one autumn day to go and see a farmer who was very ill. He was still up and about, but he had a bad cough and other ailments which were very serious. Effie found him sitting in his little parlour. It was a gloomy, dreary-looking room, and the poor farmer looked gloomy and dreary likewise. He had a great deal to say about his aches and pains, and had little hope of getting well.

Effie said she was very sorry he suffered so much, but, after all, the great matter was not whether the body was well, but whether the soul was saved. The farmer smiled in a bewildered manner, and said nothing. Then Effie talked to him about the Lord Jesus Christ, who not only healed the sick, and pitied the sorrowful, but whose heart yearned over the lost souls of men. Jesus knew that there was something worse than their sickness and suffering, namely their sin. He knew that they were just as unable to save themselves from their sin as to cure themselves of their diseases, or to raise themselves to life again when they died. And as all are born with this dreadful and hopeless disease of sin, the great question for us all is whether we have gone to the great Physician who alone can save our souls.

Then Effie told the farmer how the Lord Jesus saves sinners; that he died himself to bear the curse on them, and then having taken their punishment, he not only gives them perfect, full, free forgiveness but a new eternal life, and a place with himself in heaven.

The farmer smiled again, and moved restlessly in his chair; then he said, —

'That's all very nice for those that can understand all that sort of thing, but I never could; I never had a head for it. So it's no use to think about things one can't make head nor tail of. It's a terrible thing what a number of cows die nowadays of lung disease. Why, I've had more than a dozen ill with it, and I've lost — let me see! — how many have I lost?'

And he then took out of a drawer a large account book, and explained to Effie how much money he had lost upon the cows already, and how much more he was likely to lose.

It was plainly impossible to say anything more to him about the soul he seemed to value so little. Effie determined to try to get him to listen another day, but the next time and the next it was just the same.

'I think it very kind of you to trouble to come and talk to me,' he said, 'but it all goes over my head. Some can understand these things, and some can't. I'm one of them that can't. I'm not as good as I ought to be, no doubt, but I'll try my best.'

Then Effie explained to him that it was no use for him to try his best, for the very best he could do could never satisfy God. Therefore God took account not of our doings, but of the great work

31

done by his Son on the cross, and he was satisfied with that, and saves us on account of that, not because of anything we have done or can do.

'It's all very nice,' repeated the farmer, 'I haven't any doubt, for those who have had time to read books, and get to understand what all those things mean. But I have the farm and the cows to look after, and it isn't in my line. Thank you all the same.'

Effie was leaving the neighbourhood, and this was her last visit. She went away feeling very sad. It was a dark, damp afternoon, and the yellow leaves were lying scattered over the wet road, and the sky was dull and grey. But nothing outside the house looked to her so sad and wretched as the poor man in his dark parlour, and with his dark soul.

Six months afterwards, when Effie was in London, she got a message from the farmer, it was this —

'I know you will be glad to hear that I am saved.'

She went at once to see him. He was looking well, and his faced beamed with joy and gladness.

'I am truly glad to see you,' he said, 'I wanted to tell you that the Lord has healed my body and saved my soul.'

'Do tell me about it,' said Effie. 'How did it happen?'

'Well,' said the farmer, 'you remember last autumn, when you came to talk to me, how stupid I was?'

'Yes, I well remember,' said Effie. 'I thought you understood nothing that I said to you.'

'Yes, that's just what it was,' said the farmer. 'Well I went on just like that, dull and stupid. Sometimes I thought about what you said, and then I gave up thinking because, as I told you, I couldn't make head nor tail of it. Then, just a fortnight ago, I went to bed as dull and stupid as ever. And that night I had a dream. I dreamt that I woke, and lo and behold everything was gone! There was my room, but it was empty, and out of the window there was nothing but empty space. The cows were gone, and the crops were gone — there was nothing anywhere. And the strangest thing of all was, I was gone too! Yes, I was nowhere! I looked for myself, but I was gone, clean gone! "Well, now," I thought in my dream, "what is there left, if I'm gone, and all the rest is gone? Is there anything left? Is there anything that can't be gone?' and then, in a moment, just as if God himself had shown it me, as indeed he did, I saw that the Lord Jesus Christ remained, and that he could not be gone.

'I saw, as it were, the Lord Jesus standing alone before God, and I saw that he must be the delight of God for ever. And then in one moment all came clearly to my mind that you had said to me last autumn. I saw that it was not at me that God was looking, for I was gone. He was looking at his beloved Son, and was satisfied with him. "Yes," I said in my dream, "God is satisfied. He must be satisfied with Christ, for Christ is absolutely perfect. And I am nowhere. It is Christ himself who has satisfied God!" In my joy I awoke and I called out aloud, "I am gone and there is Christ instead of me!" Oh, what a joy it was to me and has been ever since! You see that when you used to talk to me, I kept on saying to myself, "Yes, that's all very nice, but somehow or other I must do something to satisfy God. I must repent, or pray, or turn over a new leaf, or do or feel something." I didn't know exactly what. He is perfectly satisfied with Christ. Christ has done the whole work, there is nothing to add to it. Christ stands before God for me in my place, and God looks at him, and is well pleased. Think what wonderful grace and goodness of the Lord to show me that! So ignorant and stupid as I was, I might have gone on blundering in my own way from that day to this, if the Lord himself had not come to my help. No,' he added, correcting himself, 'you see I can't even talk of it right; he didn't come to help me, he did it all himself, and I was nowhere. I see now why it was the Lord saved me in my sleep, for if I had been awake, I should have thought I had had some hand in it. Now I know he did it all. And oh, what a comfort it is to be nowhere! Only Christ, nothing but Christ, before God. What more can God want, and what more can I want?

'You see, it was not only my sin that was the trouble, but myself too. I used to think sometimes, "Well, if God did have mercy on me and forgive me, why there's myself just as bad as before. It's myself I want rid of, for I'm not fit." And now I know that old self that was such a grief and trouble is, just as it were, nowhere. God sees me no more, he looks at Christ; and it isn't a question now, "What am I?" but "What Christ is." And Christ is perfect.'

34

From that day the farmer's peace and joy seemed only to increase.

'What a comfort it is,' he said one day, 'to know that not only I am nothing, but I have nothing, nothing but Christ. I used to walk about the farm and say to myself, "Those cows are mine; those crops are mine;" and now I say to myself, "None of those things are mine." The Lord may call me away from them any moment, or take the farm from me, and then they will be nothing at all to me; but I have Christ, and I will always have Christ, and my heart is more than satisfied. If only everybody could know what it is to have Christ!'

The farmer was not content with wishing that all his neighbours might have this happiness. He spoke to them all, in season and out of season. He invited them to his house, or he went himself to find them. One of his labourers came home one evening in a state of amazement, and said to his wife, 'I've seen the strangest thing today that I ever saw. I saw our master, and yet he isn't our master, he's someone quite different. I never saw one man so different from another as he is from our old master – and yet he's the same. I can't make it out. He came right across the field to me and I wondered what for, and after all it was to speak to me about Christ, and nothing else! Why, our old master would never have gone within a mile of such matters. I looked hard, and thought, "Is it you, or isn't it?" But it was him, and it's past my comprehension.'

So the years passed and the farmer seemed to have but one grief and trouble: it was that many of his neighbours despised the good news he had to tell them, and some of his old friends even kept out of his way, and refused all invitations to come to his house. 'As long as I talked folly and nonsense to them,' he said, 'they were glad to come, but now they seem as frightened of me as if I wanted to rob them.'

So it is. People talk of being afraid of death, but they are much more afraid of life. And you, who read this, do you know what it is that God taught, in so strange a way, to the farmer? Have you ever known and believed that the Son of God himself undertook to bear all the judgment due to all your sin? Have you ever believed that he made your peace with God by the blood of his cross? Do you remember that on the resurrection day, he came to announce to his disciples that this peace was made? He came and stood in the midst and said, 'Peace be unto you.' And then he showed them his hands and his side. Then they knew how he had made the peace and that God required no more. And have you ever believed that when he had put away sin by his sacrifice he then entered heaven before you, and was welcomed to the Father's heart – and that welcome is your own?

'God is satisfied with Christ;' and all the delight of God in him, all the love of God for him, is also, if you will believe it, for you, for whom he died. How am I accepted before God? 'Accepted in the Beloved!' There is no other welcome, no other acceptance, but that of Christ, who calls to you from glory to share his joy with him, and that your joy may be full.

This joy was to the farmer as a light from heaven beyond the brightness of the sun. Effie one day said to him: 'Do you know which side of the Jordan you are?'

She only asked this question to see what he would say, for she had no idea he would understand what such a question meant. But he looked at her with wonder and said:

'Sure you needn't ask me that! How can I help knowing that I am in the land that flows with milk and honey?'

He told her that he heard Christians praying sometimes that God would forgive them, and deliver them from his wrath.

'But I couldn't do that,' he said; 'it would seem to me like a little child going on asking his mother for what she has given him already. But I can thank him that he has done it. They may blame me for this, but I can't help it. The Pharisees blamed the man who said the Lord had given him his sight, and they turned him out; but it was better to be outside with the Lord, than inside with the Scribes and Pharisees.'

One day he went to the neighbouring town to see a man who was dying, and who had just been saved.

'Good-bye,' he said, when he left him; 'you're going straight to Christ in glory, and I'm coming soon; so good-bye till we meet again.'

He then left home for some weeks, for he had relations in another country whom he had not seen for some years.

'I've never had an opportunity,' he said, 'of telling them of Christ. Perhaps I shall never have one if I don't go now whilst I can, and when I've done that I shall have nothing more on my mind.'

He came back very unwell. Not long after he sent for Effie. She found him in bed scarcely able to speak.

'Ah,' he said, 'I'm going to the Lord! Only think; perhaps in a few hours I shall be absent from the body and present with him! Think what it will be to see him face to face! I have no pain and nothing but happiness. There's only one thing I mind, and that is I can't speak loud enough to tell them all round about the love of Jesus. That's what I should like to do once more; otherwise there is nothing — nothing but happiness!'

And having said this, he knew this happiness for himself.

The Birthday Morning

It was a bright, sunny morning in June. From the window all was beautiful — the golden green meadows, the still water, and the old forest of oak and beech trees. But there was nothing so beautiful as a little child who came capering into the room, looking bright as a sunbeam. She held up her little white frock, which was filled with toys. It was her birthday morning and she was now three. She had come to show her mother the presents she had already had from brothers and sisters.

One by one she laid them on the table, and then suddenly she knelt down at her mother's dressing stool. 'O Lord Jesus,' she said, 'I do thank you for all the nice things you have given me. I thank you for my doll, for my little workbox, and for all my things. And oh, Lord Jesus, I thank you that you were punished instead of me. Amen.'

Then she got up and looked gravely at her mother and said, 'You see I 'membered about his being punished.'

She had often spoken of him before, but from this time she spoke of him continually, to all in the house, to the children with whom she played, to the village people in their cottages. And to her mother she said sometimes, 'I am going to be with Jesus. Soon I shall be gone, you will go all about the house and you will see me nowhere. There will be no Ada, but you mustn't mind, for I shall be with Jesus.'

And so it was. Nine months after that birthday morning, the Lord took her to be with himself.

It comforted her mother to write down the things she had said and how the Lord had taught her during her little life to be gentle, obedient and unselfish. But the greatest comfort was to remember her last birthday morning.

The little story was printed and translated into other languages and found its way into many strange places. The Lord had taken his little servant to be with him, but he still meant to work by her down here, in the sad, dark world out of which he had saved her. One day, at a railway station, a stranger came up to Ada's mother and said, 'You will forgive me for speaking to you, for I know you are Ada's mother, and you will be glad to hear what I am going to tell you.'

Then the lady went on to say that she had a friend, an old lady, who had always been religious and kind and conscientious, but she had never been happy. She was always frightened when she thought of dying. 'It was so terrible,' she said, 'to know that one must die, and not to know what will be afterwards! For however one may try to do one's best, one can never be sure. God must punish sin, and I have many, many sins to remember. I pray that he will forgive me, but it is an awful thought that I must one day stand before his judgment seat.'

At last one day the story of the birthday morning was given to this old lady, and her fears and her doubts passed away forever.

'For now,' she said, 'I see that Jesus has been punished instead of me, and whilst I was once afraid of dying, now I look forward to it, and am perfectly happy.'

Others also found joy and peace through the words of the little child; grown-up men and women and little children, not only those who were soon to die, but also those who wanted to show that they had passed from darkness to light, from the power of Satan unto God. Some in the slums of London, one the daughter of a thief; some in homes which the world would call bright and beautiful, but where there were hearts more dark and desolate than many in the London alleys.

In such a home, in a foreign land, a young man was dying of a terrible disease after years of suffering. 'You will be glad to hear,' a friend wrote, 'that little Ada's words seemed to come to him from heaven and to bring him perfect peace and joy. He passed away, saying that he would be happy forever with Jesus, who had died for him.'

Year after year these good tidings came, and meanwhile someone who had read the little story, wrote some simple verses, telling what the child had said on that birthday morning. Each verse ended with the blessed words that had brought peace to so many souls, 'Jesus was punished instead of me.'

About twenty years after that birthday, a little boy learnt these verses. He was taught to say them by his mother, who knew and loved the Lord Jesus. Others of the family were also believers in Jesus. But there was one who was very dear to his mother, to whom the Gospel of God was foolishness, this was her brother, who lived in the same town, and had made a boast that he never troubled himself about 'religious nonsense.' There are many people such as he was, sensible, and intelligent, and strong-minded as to the things of this world, and who feel quite sure that sound common sense is all that is needed for this life. They think that we cannot know what happens after death so they do not trouble themselves about it.

It happened that this man had a slight illness, which kept him at home for a few days. On one of these days, which was Sunday, his sister sent her little boy to see how he was. The boy found his uncle lying on the sofa. When he had given his message, his uncle said to him, 'You can stay a little and amuse me. Say me some of your poetry.'

The little boy began to repeat the verses he liked so much about little Ada.

'What is that?' his uncle said, stopping him suddenly. 'Jesus was punished instead of me?'

'Yes,' said the little boy, repeating the verse.

'What does that mean?' asked his uncle. 'Why did Ada say that?'

'She said it because it really happened,' the little boy answered. 'Jesus was punished instead.'

'How does anyone know that?' asked his uncle, looking like someone suddenly woken up to a new thought.

'It is in the Bible,' replied the child, 'mother has often told it to me.'

'I cannot believe it is in the Bible,' said the man who had so long spoken with scorn of the book he knew so little about. 'Go and fetch your mother, tell her to come to me at once and bring a Bible.'

The child obeyed, and in a short time came back with his mother.

'Is it true that it is in the Bible that Jesus was punished instead of us? I cannot believe it is there,' said her brother.

The good woman opened the Bible and read, 'Who his own self bare our sins in his own body on the tree, that we, being dead to sins, should live unto righteousness, by whose stripes ye were healed. Christ also hath once suffered for sins, the Just for the unjust, that he might bring us to God. Christ was once offered, to bear the sins of many. God hath made him to be sin for us, who knew no sin. Christ died for our sins. Christ hath redeemed us from the curse of the law, being made a curse for us. Surely he hath borne our griefs and carried our sorrows, yet we did esteem him stricken, smitten of God and afflicted. But he was wounded for our transgressions. He was bruised for our iniquities; the chastisement of our peace was upon him; and with his stripes we are healed. All we like sheep have gone astray, we have turned everyone to his own way; and the Lord hath laid on him the iniquity of us all.'

'But,' said her brother, suddenly, 'if this really happened, I can be saved!'

'It did really happen, and if you will believe it, you are saved,' replied his sister.

'It is wonderful! Why did no one ever tell me this before? Yes, he was punished instead of me – and God is satisfied!'

And from that moment the scoffing unbeliever was a new creature in Christ Jesus. He had passed from death to life. You may wonder how it was that he did not first begin to enquire whether the Bible were true. He had professed that he did not believe it, and yet he received those words into his heart without doubt or question, and was perfectly assured then, and ever afterwards, that they are the words of God. How was it that he needed no argument to prove to him that God had really said these things?

Do you think that when the blind man's eyes are opened, he needs any argument to prove to him that the sun is in the sky? When the deaf man's ears are unstopped, does he need proof that men have voices? And when God has spoken to the heart, none who have heard his voice have ever doubted again whose voice it was they heard. 'The dead shall hear the voice of the Son of God, and they that hear shall live. It is the voice that wakes the dead in a moment in the twinkling of an eye. And it had spoken to the heart of that man, so long dead in trespasses and sins.'

From that moment he was a humble and rejoicing believer in Jesus. He was soon well again, and his whole life was the proof of the great and glorious change which the voice of Christ had wrought in him. He spoke to all around of the Saviour who had died for him.

'It was Ada who taught it to me,' he said to his sister. 'I should like to know more about her. Tell me all you know.'

Then his sister gave him the little story. He read it again and again, and kept it always near him.

Four years later he became very ill. His sister went to see him and found that he was dying.

'I am going to him who died for me,' he said, 'it was that little girl who showed it to me. Bring me the little book, and put it in my hand. I want to die with that story in my hand, because it was Ada who led me to Jesus.'

And so with the book in his hand he fell asleep.

'A little child shall lead them.'

Nothing Left For You To Do

Some years ago, a dear old friend of mine went into a bookseller's shop in Germany. It was his habit to take every opportunity that came in his way of speaking of the Lord Jesus. He found the bookseller alone in his shop, and after a little talk with him, he found that he was not a believer in the gospel. He was willing, however, to listen, and the two were soon in such earnest conversation that neither of them noticed a customer, who came into the shop, and stood there waiting in silence. As soon as my old friend saw him, he drew back, and gave place to him. The customer then said to the bookseller, 'I hope that you believe what this gentleman has been saying to you, for it is the truth of God, and is taken from His blessed Word.' The customer then went on to explain in his own words, to the bookseller, what it is that Christ has done to save us, and how, by believing in Him, we are at once forgiven, and receive everlasting life.

He spoke so clearly and so earnestly, that my old friend listened with wonder and delight, for it is not common to meet with any who so simply believe the good tidings, and who are so ready to speak of Christ to others. He therefore followed the customer when he left the shop, and asked him how and where he had learnt the gospel so fully and so plainly.

'I learnt it,' answered the customer, 'just in the very last place in the world where you would have expected me to hear it;' and then, as he saw that his new acquaintance was interested, and wished to know more, he told him his story, which I will now tell you.

He was a native, he said, of North Germany, and was brought up as a Roman Catholic. Though he would always have called himself a Catholic, he had in reality no religion at all, nor had he any regard at all for right or wrong. So he spent his time in pleasing himself, as far as he could, and became so notoriously wicked that none amongst his wicked companions would have dared to sin so boldly as he did. And, strange to say, it was this extraordinary wickedness which was used by God to awaken his conscience.

It struck him one day, 'It may be true, after all, that there is an eternal punishment for sinners.' He had heard of the judgement-seat of Christ, and of the lake of fire, and he thought, 'If anyone is ever to be there, it must be myself, for I have never seen or heard of anyone who has sinned as I have done.'

He was still quite young, and till now he had delighted in his sinful life, but this thought so terrified him that he suddenly left his wicked companions and gave himself up to despair. Sometimes he thought of all the means by which he had heard that sinners could be saved. He knew that some went into monasteries, and did penances, and a faint hope arose within him that by that means it might be just possible to escape eternal punishment, and have in exchange, perhaps some thousands of years of purgatory. But to gain such a favour from God it would be necessary to do more penances than anyone had ever done before.

He knew of no monastery where the rule would be strict enough. In most of them the monks appeared to live comfortable lives, and have plenty of the good things of this world. What could he do? He heard at last of a place which it was said had a rule more severe than any other in the world. It was in Sicily, and belonged to monks of the order of La Trappe.

In case you should not have heard of these monks, I must explain to you what sort of life they lead. They get up at a quarter-to-two. On grand festivals they get up at midnight. They have services in the chapel, or in their cells, till seven. They then go out to work in the fields. Their work is very hard and wearisome, but neither heat nor cold, rain nor storm make any difference. Nor may they alter their dress according to the weather; their thick woollen clothes must be worn all day and all night, never taken off or washed.

At half-past ten they have a very little bread, with a little water and vegetables. Only twelve ounces of food, and twelve of water, are allowed for each one during the whole day. Afterwards, till five in the evening, they have services, they read, they work in the garden. Then they have two ounces of bread and a little water, in the dining-hall, which is hung with pictures of corpses, skeletons, and souls in purgatory.

There are services and reading till eight, then they go to lie down on some hard knotted straw ropes, which are called a bed. If anyone is very ill and likely to die, this hard bed is exchanged for a layer of dust and ashes on the brick floor. They may never speak except for an hour on Sundays. They may then say a few words on religious matters.

None may work near to one another. None may give any hint as to their names or age, or past history.

One poor young monk died of the hardships he underwent. About a year after, the old monk who nursed him in silence when he was dying, was seen standing with his arms folded, looking at his gravestone. But no one spoke a word, and no one knew why he looked so earnestly at the gravestone till ten years after; then he too died, and his name was put on his gravestone. The monks knew from that time that the young monk was his son.

So far is the rule for each day and for all alike. But besides this, each one may add to his hardships and sufferings, as his conscience directs. One will wear a knotted rope, tightly fastened round his waist, till it wears away his skin. Another will beat himself with a scourge to which pointed bits of iron are fastened. Another will mix mud or dust with his water, or lick the dust from the floor. It is not difficult to invent tortures, but it is impossible ever to invent any that will silence the guilty conscience. So the long years pass by, and peace and rest seem as far off as at first.

When the young German heard of this monastery he determined to go at once and offer himself to the monks. He was poor, and the long journey would be expensive; he, therefore, made up his mind to walk, begging his way as he went. This would be the beginning of his penance. It was a walk of many hundred miles, and many months were needed for it.

He found himself at last crossing the Straits of Messina, and then there was but little more walking to do before he reached the old monastery, with its grey walls and gloomy towers. He was very tired and worn out by the time he stood at the little gate and rang the bell. The gate was slowly opened by a very old monk, who seemed scarcely able to move. The old man asked him what he wanted.

'I want to be saved,' replied the German. The old monk looked kindly at him, and led him into a little room near the gate, where they were alone together.

'Now, tell me what you mean,' said the old man. 'I should like to hear your history.'

The young German told his sad story.

'I have been a far greater sinner,' he said, 'than anyone I ever heard of. I do not think it possible that I can be saved. But anything that can be done I am willing to do, if only I may have a faint hope at last that I may, perhaps, escape the eternal punishment; but it must be by spending all the rest of my life in penance, and the harder it is the more I shall be thankful if I may do it. Only tell me what I am to do, and I will do it gladly.'

'If you will do what I tell you,' replied the old monk, 'you will go back to Germany, for there has been One down here who has done the whole work in your place before you came, and He has finished it; He did it instead of you, so that there is nothing left for you to do. It is all done.'

The young German knew not what to make of these wonderful words.

'Who has done it?' he asked.

'Did you never hear of the Lord Jesus Christ?' asked the old man.

'Yes, of course I have heard of Him.'

'Do you know where He is?' said the old man.

'Yes, of course I know. He is in heaven,' replied the German.

'But tell me,' said the old man, 'do you know why He is in heaven?'

'No, except that He is always in heaven.'

'He was not always in heaven,' said the old man. 'He came down here to do the work that you want to do yourself: He came down here to bear the punishment of your sin. He is in heaven now, because the work is done. If it were not so, He would still be here, for He came down to put away sin by the sacrifice of Himself.

'Do you not know what he has said upon the cross "It is finished"? What was finished? It was the work you want to begin. And now,' added the old monk, 'if you want to add the crowning sin to your wicked life, and to do something worse than all that you have done before, you may stay here and cast contempt upon the blessed, perfect work

51

of the Son of God, and take upon yourself to do what he only could do, and what he has done and finished. It will be as much as saying "Christ has not done enough, and I must add to the work that He has declared is finished."

'It may seem strange to you that I stay here where Christ is thus insulted, but I am very old and I can only walk to the gate. I cannot get away, so I must stay here till the Lord calls me hence. But you can go, and I entreat you to go back at once to your friends, and to tell them all that the Lord has done for you. You may stay here three days, and I will tell you all I can during that time about the Lord Jesus, and then you must go.'

'And so,' said the German, when he had finished his strange story, 'I did remain there three days, and the old man told me much more of the work of the Lord Jesus. He told me not only what His death had done for me, but how He had risen again to give me eternal life, and how He had won for me a place in heaven above the angels, where He is waiting for me and for all who believe in Him. And so I came back to Germany, and from that day to this, I have told any who will listen, the blessed news of the perfect work of Christ.'

No more could be known of the old monk but his blessed words may yet bring peace to many souls, as they did to the young German who was the chief of sinners.

The Story of Cécile

One summer evening, some years ago, I was sitting under an oak tree with a dear old friend. He had been for many years a minister of the gospel, but before that he had been in the army, and had had many strange adventures. He had been with the great Duke of Wellington in Spain, and he had been afterwards at the battle of Waterloo. He was a beautiful old man, with snow-white hair, which was to him a crown of glory, for he had long been walking in the ways of righteousness. Had you only seen his bright and happy face you would have known he must be a very pleasant companion. And could you have heard the stories he had to tell of the wonderful ways in which God had led him, you would understand why I was so glad to spend the evening listening to him. So I began by saying, 'Do tell me a story.' And he said, 'I will tell you the story of Cécile.' He thought for a few moments, as though his memory had to travel back to a time very long ago, and then he began his story as you shall now hear it.

'After the battle of Waterloo,' he said, 'the English and Prussians marched, as you know, to Paris. We English were in great spirits, and we expected we were to enter Paris in triumph the moment we arrived there. But this was not to be. It seems that a good many of Napoleon's old officers were still in Paris, and it was feared that they would raise riots to insult the British soldiers on their entrance. So it was thought necessary first to get them all cleared out of the way, and for this reason we had to wait outside Paris for several days. We knew that there were a great many Parisians who would be only too glad to welcome us, for there were still very many who were warmly attached to the family of the old Bourbon Kings, and who were delighted that we had beaten Napoleon. They looked upon us as their deliverers, for they quite understood we were willing that the princes of the old family should be restored. There was one part of Paris which was chiefly inhabited by the families of the old nobility, who were rejoicing in the thought of seeing us march in.

'I was a harum-scarum young fellow in those days, and it was a great trial to my patience to have to wait outside Paris when I longed for a happy life amongst the friendly Parisians. So one day I said to a friend of mine, "Suppose you and I put on plain clothes, and ride off into Paris as soon as it gets dark. We could stay all night and get back tomorrow morning before we are found out." My friend was quite ready for this little expedition, so we started off without being seen, saw all sorts of sights, and had plenty of fun, and went to sleep at an hotel. But next morning, just as we were at breakfast, the news came that Paris was all astir, for the British army was to march in that very day. We sprang upon our horses, hoping to get back in time. We saw the tricolour flag already hauled down from the

Tuileries, and the old white standard flying. And as we came to the Porte S. Denis, there we saw the English troops already marching in. Of course we had no desire to meet them, so we turned round and took another road, which would lead us to the camp by a longer way round. We had to ride all the length of a long and narrow street in which several of the old noble families had their houses. We found a carriage standing in this street before the door of a large house, and as the street was so narrow, we had to wait behind it till it had driven off before we could go further. The party from the house were just taking their places in the carriage.

'How little I knew that our arriving just at that moment was part of a great plan which God had made for the glory of His beloved Son! But so it was to turn out in the end. In those days I had no thoughts of God, and cared only to live a merry life, without looking forward to the end of it.

'As we waited behind the carriage we saw the family get in; three ladies first — plainly a mother and two daughters — and then a gentleman. I pulled up my horse, of course, and lifted my hat as the ladies passed. The last one who got in was the youngest. She seemed about sixteen or seventeen years old. She sat with her back to the horses, so she had her face towards me. She was very lovely, with a sweet, bright expression that charmed me at once. All the ladies were dressed in white, and each had a white rosette fastened on her dress. As the carriage drove off I cantered by the side of it, and said, "May I ask if you are going to meet our

British soldiers?" "Indeed we are," said the elder lady, "and gladly too." Then I said, "I would like to show my loyalty to the Bourbon King, but I have no white rosette. Might I ask if the young lady would give me hers?" The young lady at once unpinned it, but her mother stopped her. I saw that I had asked too much, and I cantered on after my friend, covering my disappointment with a joke. At the end of the street we found we had to wait again, for the way was blocked with wagons. The carriage stopped too. I saw the gentleman get out and beckon to me. I rode up to him and he told me politely that the lady in the carriage was a noble woman and that she begged me to accept the rosette from herself. She did not wish her young daughter to give it to me, but at the same time she wished to show her good feeling towards an Englishman. I was of course much pleased, and I asked whether the noble lady lived in the house at the door of which the carriage had been standing, for I hoped to call one day to thank her. A day or two later my friend and I went to call there. The marquise received us very kindly. She told us she was a widow with two daughters and a young son. She wished to know a little more about us, as of course we were perfect strangers to her. She seemed quite satisfied with the account we gave of ourselves. Soon the two daughters came in. Laure, the eldest, was handsome and pleasant-looking, but Cécile, the youngest, was more beautiful than anyone I had ever seen. She was very graceful, and her sweet and pleasant manners very soon won my heart completely. She was very simple and child-like, but at the same time she was clever and intelligent, and very modest and gentle. I found all this out from many visits which I paid to the family. She was allowed to take walks with me, and her mother seemed fully to understand that I had become very fond of her daughter, and to be pleased that so it was.

'It grieved me very much that I had suddenly to leave Paris a few weeks later. Business called me to London, where I had to spend some time. I had not asked leave to write to Cécile, and I often longed to hear something about her. One day I did hear something, and terrible news it was. I received from Cécile's mother a printed paper, such as the French usually send to their friends to give notice of a death or a marriage in a family. This notice was of a marriage. Cécile was engaged to a German nobleman, to whom she was to be married immediately. I heard afterwards how it had come about. Just after I left Paris, a concert was given in honour of the King of Prussia, who had arrived there with his army. The concert room was crowded; the heat was very great, and Cécile fainted away. There was a moment of confusion; it was difficult to make a way to take Cécile out of the room. The king sent his aide-de-camp, a tall Prussian officer, to see what was the matter. The officer at once took Cécile in his arms, and carried her into a private room. The king ordered his carriage to take home the marquise and her daughters. Next day the aide-de-camp called to ask after Cécile. After this he called again and again; and before a month was over the marquise had gladly allowed him to consider Cécile as engaged to him. French girls were not supposed to have any will of their own in these matters. It was settled for them by fathers or mothers, and as a matter of course they were to obey. So Cécile married the aide-de-camp and returned with him to Berlin. The news reached me that she was much admired there. And then I heard no more. I was very unhappy. If I could but have seen her to say good-bye, I thought it would have comforted me. But now she was gone for ever, and I said to myself, "I shall never see her again, or know anything about her!"

'So the years passed by. I tried to forget her, and so I gave myself up to a life of pleasure. I had many friends who were fond of my company. I could sing and dance well, and play on the guitar, and tell them of strange places and strange things which I had seen in foreign countries. English people did not travel about the world in those days as they do now, and many things were new to them which everybody now knows all about.

'So the time went on. Visiting in the morning; balls, music, theatres at night. If I had any spare time I wrote poetry, and plays, and novels. It never struck me that all these precious years were wasted and lost, or worse than lost, for if we are not gathering with Christ, we are scattering abroad. That is to say, we are either doing Christ's work or Satan's. But at last a time came when God opened my blind eyes, and I saw myself to be a lost, guilty sinner, walking in the broad road which has only one ending — everlasting destruction. And, thanks be to God, I saw also that there is a Saviour, one only Saviour for lost sinners.

'How true it is that no one can teach this to our hearts but God Himself, God the Holy Spirit. How good He was to teach it me! I had been living without Him, and had not gone to Him for comfort and happiness, but to the foolish, useless pleasures which after all had never satisfied me. And now I saw it all clearly, that Christ Jesus on the cross had won for me a happiness that could never be taken away from me. He had given me life, and peace, and rest that were all new to me, and everything round me seemed changed. I could now thank Him that He had not allowed me to have Cécile for my wife. At the time when I had known her, it mattered nothing to me whether people trusted in Jesus, or in saints and angels. Now I saw what the difference is between those who own the Lord Jesus as the one only Saviour, and those who think that it needs also their works and prayers, and the help of saints and angels to open to them the door of heaven. I saw that the door had been opened by the Lord Himself when He died upon the cross, and I knew that I had entered in, and that I was saved. But though my heart was comforted and I was unspeakably happy, I had not forgotten Cécile. I longed that she too might know the Lord Jesus, and be as happy as I was. I had often prayed, even before my blind eyes were opened, that God would make her happy. But it was the happiness of this world I had meant when I prayed for her in those days. Now I asked

59

the Lord to show her Jesus, and to save her soul. I felt sure He would hear me, though years upon years passed by, and I never had any tidings of her. Ten, twenty, thirty, forty years had passed at last, and still there was scarcely ever a day that I did not pray for Cécile.

'Meanwhile I had been preaching and working for my Master, and at last I became worn out, and I wanted rest. A kind friend, who was a doctor, said he would go with me to Italy. Three months' rest were allowed me, and a sum of money was given me to pay all my expenses. At Rome my friend left me, and then I went on alone to Milan, and to beautiful, old Venice.

'I wished very much to see some of the great German cities on my way back. It seemed to me it would be a great pleasure to wander through the old towns where Luther had lived and preached. And so I began to measure the time that was left, and to count my money. I found that I would have just enough of both to last me till I got to England, if only I wasted no time on the road. I meant to allow myself one day at Leipzig, to see the place where the great battle of Leipzig had been fought, two years before Waterloo. But it is God who orders all our steps, and the smallest things that happen to us are a part of His great plan. Our plans have often to be altered or given up, that His plan may be carried out. And so it happened that when I got to Leipzig it rained in torrents, and I had already passed over the battlefield in the train, so I determined to go to Berlin without further delay. Many of the

Lord's servants were just at that time holding great meetings at Berlin. There were some from almost every country in Europe, and many of my English friends were amongst them. I went to one of the meetings, but all that was said was in German, and I did not understand it. So I went out and walked down the great street called Unter den Linden. All at once the thought struck me, "I wonder if Cécile is still alive!" I tried to remember the exact name of her husband, but I could not be sure of it. I went into a bookseller's shop, and asked for the Berlin directory. I looked out the names that seemed to be nearest to the name I had once known so well. There were seven names something like it. I could not be sure which it was. However, I wrote them down, and then went to three of the houses named in the directory. But I could hear of no one who could possibly be Cécile. So I thought it was foolish of me to think more about it. Just as I left the last house, I met an English friend, who said to me, "Are you not going with us to the King?" "What do you mean?" I said, "Why should I go to the King?" My friend explained that the King had invited all the foreigners who had come over to the meetings, to be received by him in his new palace at Potsdam. There was to be a special train for them from Berlin to Potsdam, which was to start at two o'clock.

'"You have only to show your ticket," said my friend, for all those who had gone to Berlin for the meetings had what were called conference tickets. "I have no ticket," I said. I was sorry I had none, for I wished to go with the rest. They told me if

I went to an office in the city, I might get one. I went there at once, and I met the gentleman who gave the tickets, just coming downstairs. I told him what I wanted. He said, "It is too late." But when I mentioned my name, he ran back and found a ticket for me, "though," he said, "most likely I shall miss the train by getting it for you." I drove him off to the station in my droschke, that is the German name for a cab. The whistle was sounding, the train had already moved off, but we jumped into a carriage just as the guard was shutting the door, and we arrived at Potsdam.

'The King received us on the terrace. There were nearly 1200 people there. I saw that it would be a very long ceremony, so I made my way out of the crowd, and found myself close to a Prussian officer. I said to him, "Do you know General L.?" This was one of the seven names I had seen in the directory. "Ah," he said, "you mean General von L.," altering the name a little. Yes, that was the name, I remembered it well now. "Is he alive?" I said. "Yes, he is quite an old man now," replied the officer. "He married a French lady a long time ago, who is a great deal at the court." So Cécile was alive. "Where do they live?" I asked. "Quite near," he said, "it is a house on that hill just outside the park; it is called Vicsberg."

"I took leave of my Prussian friend, and started at once on my way to Vicsberg. I did not stop to look at the beautiful palace gardens through which I had to pass, but I walked on quickly, praying earnestly in my heart to the Lord, that He might show me how best to speak to Cécile of the blessed work of Christ. I found some droschkies waiting outside the park, and I told the driver to take me at once to the house of General von L. Very soon he drew up at an iron gate, which opened on a lawn in front of a large house. I asked the servant who opened the door if the lady was at home. He said she was. I bade him say that a gentleman wished to see her, but I did not give my name. The man took me into the drawing-room, and lighted the lamps, for it was getting dark. I stood there waiting. A door at the end of the room opened, and a lady came in, who stooped, and seemed to be an invalid. She asked me politely, "Whom have I the honour of receiving?" I said, "Do you remember the day when the British army entered Paris?" She looked up at me, clasped her hands, and said, "Most certainly! You are Alexander!" And she began at once to remind me of a thousand things that had happened in those old days, and she asked me many questions about my life since then. She told me she had five sons and two daughters; one was a widow, the other was living at home. "You shall see her," she said, and she went across the room to ring the bell.

'This was the first moment of silence, and I thought, "If I do not speak to her now and at once, of the Lord Jesus, I may have no other opportunity." I had meant to do so by degrees, but I saw that this would be impossible. So I said at once, "Cécile, I used to love you very dearly in those old days, but I love you a great deal more now." She stopped and looked up at me. "Yes," I said, "it was my natural

63

heart that loved you then. But now I love you for your soul's sake. I long that you may be saved." "What do you mean?" she asked. "Cecile," I said, "a great change has happened to me, since you knew me in the old days." And I went on to tell her what great things the Lord had done for me; that He had saved me, and forgiven me; that He had given me a new life, and had put His Spirit into me, and had sent me out to tell others of His great salvation. "For thirty years," I said, "He has given me that glorious work to do. I know now how wrong is the teaching that you have had from your priests, and how true it is that only in God's holy Word can we find the truth that saves us." As I was speaking, the door gently opened, and Cécile said, "Come in, Loulou, and see an old and dear friend of mine; who do you think it is?" A nice, pleasant-looking girl came forward, saying, "How can I tell, mother?" Her mother said, "Think, Loulou — a very dear friend." "Ah!" Loulou said, "can it be Mr. D.?" "Yes, you have guessed," said her mother.

'Then Loulou took the hand I held out to her, and kissed it, and said, "I am very glad indeed to see you." I wished to lose no more of the precious time which remained to speak of Christ. So I again began to tell Cécile more about His love and grace. But now that Loulou was there listening, Cécile seemed unwilling to speak. I felt that I could say no more till I had a better opportunity.

'It was getting late, and I had but little time to catch the train for Berlin. Cécile begged me to come again next day. I said I had promised to spend that day with some friends, but would come the day after. So on that day I again appeared, and found Cécile alone in the drawing room. She said dinner was not yet over, but that she had done, and was glad to have some more talk with me. I took out my French Testament, and wrote her name in it. I entreated her to promise me that she would read it carefully, and I said, "Remember, Cécile, it is only God the Holy Spirit who can teach you to understand it." I then asked her if Loulou was a Roman Catholic. "Of course she is," she said, all my children are." I said, "I hope I may be able to teach her better."

'Just then Loulou came in from the dining-room. I said to her, "My dear child, I have been making a present to your mother, and I have got one for you." I put into her hand another New Testament, and I wrote her name in it, telling her it was the book of God. Two young men now came in, and I thought it might be best to leave. I said I had a droschke waiting at the gate. "Oh, send it away," said Cecile, "my carriage shall take you to any train you like, later in the day." So I went to tell the driver not to wait, and whilst I was trying to make out what fare he asked, Loulou came to me and said, "My mother sent me to speak to the driver for you, as you don't understand German."

'The matter was soon settled, and the man drove away. Then Loulou turned to me, and said to me these words, which I shall never forget: – "Mr. D., it was God who sent you here, just at the moment when I needed it so greatly. I have long known that the Roman Catholic teaching is false. I can no longer bear to be a hypocrite. I have gone on till now calling myself a Roman Catholic, when in my heart I am not one. But I do not know what to do. I fear it would kill my dear mother if I left the Church of Rome, and yet I cannot bear to go to mass. The day before yesterday, just before you came, I spoke to the only friend who knows my secret, and we joined together in prayer that God would make a way for me. My friend advised me to tell my mother all, and I made up my mind to do so, though it was dreadful to me to think of grieving her so deeply; it made me so ill to think about it, that I had to leave dinner, and go to my room. Just then a servant came to tell me that my mother wanted me to see a friend. I said "I am too unwell to go down." And yet when I had said that, I felt that I must go. I knew not why, but I could not help it. I opened the drawing-room door gently, and I heard my mother say to you, "I respect those people who act according to their conscience in matters of religion." That encouraged me. So I went in, and I was pleased when I found that my mother's friend was yourself, for she had so often told me about you. I imagined you were an officer in the army. But when you began to speak to my mother about the Lord Jesus, and I found you were a minister of the gospel — oh! I cannot tell you what I felt at that moment."

'Loulou and I walked about the garden for a long time. My heart overflowed with thankfulness to find that the Lord had thus guided me, and shown me His hand in the whole of this matter.

'I had but little opportunity of saying more to Cécile that evening. I was obliged to leave Berlin next day to return to England, so I saw my dear friend no more. But Loulou had promised to write to me, and she did so. She told me that her mother had shown no displeasure when she heard that Loulou was no longer a Roman Catholic. And when her brothers heard of this, two of them told Loulou that they had for years been longing to leave the Church of Rome, but had not dared to do so for the sake of their mother. Now they both came forward boldly, and all three together made an open profession of the gospel.

'And the wonder was that their mother seemed also to be entirely changed. She said not a word to oppose them. She daily read the New Testament, and a strange peace and joy seemed to fill her heart. She spoke but little, for, from the time of my visit to Potsdam, she had never been well. She grew weaker each day, and died two months after our last meeting. From all that Loulou told me in her letters of her mother's last days, I feel sure that she was trusting simply and only to the Lord Jesus, and that she departed to be with him. Loulou sent me back the Testament with the marker in it where her mother had last been reading. Soon after this the dear child married a Protestant officer, and she has now three little girls, whom she is training up for Christ.

'I have often thought over all the steps in this wonderful history. I have marked the blessed ways of God who ordered all my goings. Had I stopped a day at Leipzig as I intended, I should have been too late for the visit to Potsdam. Had I not met my friends at the street corner, just in time to tell me of the special train, or had I been a moment later at the office, and missed the secretary, I should not have gone there. Had I not been led to look for Cécile's name in the directory, I could not have found my way to Vicsberg. And on all these little circumstances, then, depended a visit which was to bring eternal life to Cécile, and blessing and peace to her children.'

This was my old friend's story. Not long after he too departed to be with Christ, and to all eternity will he and Cécile rejoice in the answer to forty years of prayer.

Part Two

Amy's Story

The first time I saw Amy was on a summer afternoon, when I went with my mother to pay a visit to some people who lived by the park. The house was pleasant and large and situated where there were shady woods of fine old oaks, and large ponds full of reeds and white water-lilies. As we were talking to the lady of the house a little girl came in, who had a round rosy face, and large grey eyes, that were both very dark and very bright. Her hair was cut short, like a boy's. She was dressed in a print frock, with a white pinafore. She seemed to be about six or seven years old. This was Amy. I often saw Amy after this, for her sister, who was ten years older, became a great friend of mine, and my little sister became a great friend of Amy's, and of her sister Fanny, who was a year or two older. Amy lived in the house with her sisters and mother but with no father. Amy had no father, and could never remember having a father.

But for some time I took little notice of Amy, because I was so much older than she was. At last I began to be very much interested in her. I don't know why one is more interested in the wild and mischievous children than in the steady ones. Perhaps you can find a reason for it. Amy's sister, Maria, used to call her the Wild Rose, and the tall, quiet, well-behaved Fanny, the White Lily. The

Wild Rose would, in any other family, have been in constant scrapes, but Amy's mother liked her children to do as they pleased, and nobody asked Amy where she had been, or what she had been doing, when she drove the farm carts, or climbed on the roof of the gardener's cottage, and slid down into a haystack at the back. 'Did she do no lessons?' you say. Yes, sometimes, when she liked. And she did like some of her lessons, for she was very clever, and fond of reading, especially poetry. She was also very fond of arithmetic. So she managed to escape being altogether a dunce. But a time came, when Amy was about eight years old, that it was found needful to look after her a little more closely. My little sister was found one day taking a letter all alone to the post. The village in which we lived was about six miles distant from Amy's home, and the little girls often wrote to one another. My sister's letter was directed to Amy. It was, as far as I can remember, as follows:

'My dear Amy,
I will meet Fanny and the ponies in the road,
as you told me, at four o'clock in the morning.
It will be great fun to live in the wood.
I am, your affectionate
Carrie.'

What could this mean? Little Carrie thought it was best to tell the whole story.

Amy had long thought that to live in a house was far less pleasant than to live out of doors in a wood. She had, therefore, made up her mind to run away, and to live in the oak woods at the farther end of the large park. She considered that an unused boat, with a few wraps and cushions, would make a first-rate bed. As for food, Amy began, like a squirrel, to store up an ample provision. Every morning at breakfast she slipped one or two pieces of toast under her pinafore. She also managed, now and then, to stow away figs, raisins, almonds and biscuits. But the fun of living in the wood would be much greater if she had some friends to talk to. She, therefore, took Fanny, and her friend Carrie, into the secret; and they, too, had been for some time hoarding up toast and biscuits. As for drink, Amy assured them that she could climb in and out of the dairy window by night with the greatest ease, as she had practised doing so; and she had provided herself with a large jug, which would hold milk enough for the whole party for a whole day.

All this being arranged, Amy had written to Carrie to say that she and Fanny would get the stable key, and harness the two little ponies in the middle of the night. Fanny would ride one and lead the other, and would arrive at a certain turn in the road in the village at four o'clock in the morning. There Carrie was to meet her, and return with her on the black pony to the oak wood, where Amy would be waiting to receive them, with the jug of milk and the store of toast. The ponies were to live with them in the wood. It was a great grief to Amy and to Carrie that this fine plan was knocked on the head. I rather think that it was a relief to Fanny to find that she was still to sleep in a comfortable bed, and have her pleasant schoolroom to live in, and her breakfast, dinner and tea at the right time and in the proper manner. After this Amy's mother kept an eye on her proceedings, but Amy was still allowed to do a great many things which other little girls would never dream of doing, or of wishing to do.

All this time I was only amused with Amy's antics, and I did not consider her very naughty. I remembered the time when I, too, would have liked to live in a wood and sleep in a boat. But a day came when I began to think that there was something worse about Amy than her wild ways, and doing things which she did not like her mother to know.

I ought to tell you that at that time I very seldom thought about the Lord Jesus Christ, for I grieve to say I had never believed in his great love to me, and therefore when I thought of him it was not with love but with fear, and of course one thinks as little as one can about anything which makes one afraid. So it did not make me unhappy to find that Amy knew nothing about the Lord Jesus, and never cared about him or wished to please him. But there was something that made me unhappy.

I was busy one summer's evening in my room, which was at the top of the tall house in which we lived. The window was shut at the bottom, but wide open at the top. Amy, who was then staying with us, and who very much wanted to be my friend, came into my room, but I was too busy to notice what she was about. At last, on looking round, I saw her standing on the narrow window-sill outside the window. She had climbed over the two sashes. As far as I can remember, I had enough sense left in my terrified mind not to speak, or to rush at her. I went very quietly and softly to the window, got on a chair, and before Amy was aware of it I had seized her firmly by the arms. I cannot tell you how I managed to drag her in, but I succeeded in doing so. Amy now flew at me in a fit of wild passion. She beat me, kicked me, and even bit me, and poured out a stream of bad names, and of such terrible bad language, as I had never heard before. Perhaps she had learnt it from the farm boys, with whom she drove in hay-carts.

I took her down into the garden, and at last sent her to have a run in the large paddock, that she might forget her anger. But I could not forget Amy's bad words, and the hatred, which she now seemed to feel for me, though I had perhaps saved her life.

It had been something quite new to her that anyone should interfere with her wishes, and she had been at the height of happiness when she stood on the window-sill, looking down on the tops of the trees in the garden below.

I found out other things, at this time, which convinced me that Amy was not merely wild, but a thoroughly naughty child. And yet there was still a charm about her. It was sad to think of the little Wild Rose as a wild bramble or a thistle.

Soon after this Amy's mother left England, and went to live in the beautiful valley of the Neckar, near Heidelberg, in Germany. So I saw no more of the Wild Rose, and heard no more of her for several long years.

During those years I began to find out something, which grieved and astonished me far more than Amy's naughtiness. I found out — or rather, God showed me — the wickedness of my own heart. I came to see that, though I had never said such bad words as Amy had said, I was still a bad, lost, helpless sinner. Was I as bad as Amy? Most likely I was much worse. I felt that I was too bad for God to love me and too helpless to make myself any better. I was, therefore, too unhappy to think much of anything else; for a time I forgot Amy, or, if I thought of her, I said to myself, 'I am worse than she is.'

I am thankful to tell you that God then showed me something more: something so wonderful, and so beautiful, and so sweet, that for a time I could scarcely think of anything else. He showed me that he loved me just as I was - bad and helpless! He showed me that the Lord Jesus had suffered on the cross the punishment of all my sins — of all, all my sins — so that nothing remained for which God would ever punish me. But the best part of this great message from God was not that there was no punishment for me; the best part was the reason why the Lord Jesus himself had been punished instead of me. Why had he died in agony upon the cross, with all my sins upon his head? It was because God the Father so loved me that he sent his Son to save me — me, wicked as I was. It was because God the

Son so loved me that he delighted to do the will of God in dying for me. And God the Spirit brought this great message to my heart. I read it with my eyes in the Bible, but my heart saw it by the great power of the Spirit. He opens the blind eyes of the heart to see the love of God and the God of love. So now I became happy — I cannot tell you how happy. And then I thought again of the poor little Wild Rose, and I wondered whether she too would ever know the Lord Jesus and his wonderful love to sinners.

Soon after this, a friend who came from Germany, brought me some news of Amy. She was now thirteen years old. She had grown tall and slender, and had begun to study a great deal in her own way, chiefly languages and mathematics. She also liked to read anything about the ways and means for making poor people better off and happier.

Amy felt quite convinced, from all she read and from all she saw, that the misery and poverty of the poor was mostly caused by drink. Now I would not contradict anybody who says that all kinds of misery and wretchedness are caused by drink. But we must think further: what is it that causes the drink? If you had a fever and lost your senses, and did harm to people, we ought to try to find out not only how the fever can be cured, but how the thing can be cured that causes the fever. Perhaps there is some well of bad, dirty water about the place which makes people have fevers?

It is true that there is something in you and in me, and in all men, women and children, which is like a well of bad water. To some people it gives the fever of drunkenness, to some of selfishness, to some of spite and bad temper. And if that well could be stopped, the drunkenness and spite and bad temper would be at an end. Do you know what I mean? Out of the evil heart come all the evil ways.

But Amy did not understand this. She was not concerned about the evil hearts of the poor drunkards around her, but she was very sorry for their rags and their misery, and for their ragged, starving wives and children. That was right, but it was only a small part of the matter.

Amy did not end, as most people do, in being sorry for drunkards. She determined that she at least would do something to cure them of drinking. She, therefore, made acquaintance with as many of the men and boys in the villages round Heidelberg as she could possibly get at. She talked to them in a friendly way, and did any little kindness for them that she was able to do. Everyone liked Amy, and these men and boys became devoted to her. Then Amy began little by little to talk to them about the drink, and to get them to promise not to go to the beer and wine shops.

Every day she would set off with a large dog, and walk through the villages within a few miles of her home. She would stop at every beershop and look in the door, or watch the people who came to drink at the little tables under the shady trees outside. If she saw any of the people that she knew, she would walk boldly up to them and say, 'Karl' or 'Fritz,' 'you know quite well you have no business here: and I shall wait for you till you come home. But I am sure you will come home at once, to please me.' Then Karl or Fritz would get up and look rather silly and walk away. Once or twice boys who met her in her walks would try to be rude, but the great dog soon settled that matter, and sent them flying over the hedges and ditches, though Amy would never allow him to really hurt them. His great bark was enough.

When Amy was fourteen her mother came back to England; but it was not to their old home. It was in fact a long way off, so I did not see Amy for some time. Her new home was about a mile from Bath, on the beautiful hills near Avon. There were woods round the house, to which poachers used to come as soon as it was getting dark. Amy's brothers were not often at home, and her eldest sister had married in Germany, so now only Amy and Fanny were left. Amy considered herself the protector of her mother and sister. She was not one of those girls who liked to talk schoolboy slang, and behave like boys; but at the same time she had learnt to do most things that boys can do, in case it should be of use to her to know how to do them. She could harness a horse and load and fire a gun, but few people would have remarked that she was anything but a quiet, grave girl, fond of books and of her own company.

One evening, when everybody was out, she observed some men in the woods, and felt sure they were poachers. She followed them and found that she had not wrongly suspected them.

'You have no business here,' she said, 'and the sooner you are off the premises the better for you.'

The men were amazed, and one of them in fun pointed this gun at her.

'I can pull a trigger as well as you,' said Amy, coolly, 'and I strongly advise you to be off.'

The men thought it best to take her advice; and, having seen them safely over the park railings, she returned home.

Soon after this, she was sitting alone in her little study; her mother had given her a little room upstairs, where she might learn mathematics without being disturbed.

It was a hot summer's night, about ten o'clock, and the window, which looked out on a balcony over the garden, was wide open. It was Amy's habit to study all the evening, and she was always allowed to do just as she pleased about this and everything else. On this evening Amy was roused from her studies by the sound of two voices in the garden. One was a man's voice, loud and gruff; the other was a woman's voice, upset and crying. Amy went out on the balcony; nothing was to be seen but the black masses of the trees, for the night was very dark. The voices became louder. In a moment Amy had climbed the railing of the balcony, and, by the aid of the creepers, had let herself down into the garden below. She went across the lawn, in the direction of the voices. A white object was to be seen by the light of the stars near the little side gate, which led into the road. Amy went straight up to this white figure, which proved to be one of the maids in her light print gown; she was crying bitterly. A man, who was standing in the road, moved away as Amy came up, and went down the hill towards Bath.

'Who is that?' enquired Amy.

'It is my father, Miss,' said the maid; 'and oh, Miss, he's not fit to go home by himself, for he's been drinking, and he can't walk steady, and he'll have to go all along the narrow path by the side of the river. He lives in Avon Street, Miss, and he'll have a mile to go in the dark.'

'But you ought to go with him,' said Amy. 'Run after him as fast as you can and take him home, and come back tomorrow morning; I will tell my mother where you are gone.'

'Oh no, Miss,' said the maid; 'you don't know what father's like when he's had the drink! None of my family dares to go near him. He'd knock me down and half kill me. But oh! Father will be drowned! And what am I to do?'

'Will you go?' repeated Amy.

'No, Miss – I dare not. I couldn't go near him, Miss.'

'Then I must go,' said Amy, and in a moment she had disappeared in the darkness down the hill.

She soon overtook the man, to whom she said, 'John, I am going to walk home with you. So come on, and let me walk this side of you, next to the river. And now, John, walk as steadily as you can.'

John growled, but made no further objection. Several times he reeled half-over, but Amy managed to keep him on his legs, and in course of time they arrived at the door of his wretched house in Avon Street.

Till now the man had not spoken a word, but the sight of his wife and children through the open door seemed to suddenly rouse him into fury. He sprang into the room with a shout of rage. The poor woman, with the screaming children, fled into the farthest corner of the room, and cowered down on the floor in the darkness. The man seized a chair, the only one in the room, and hurled it after them. The chair struck the wall, and fell to the ground in splinters, but none of them were hurt.

'Go up to bed,' said Amy to the woman; 'take the children with you, and leave him to me.'

The woman obeyed, and speedily vanished up the ladder staircase.

Amy took the man by both hands and said, 'Sit down, John.' She looked round for a chair, but as there was none, she said, 'Sit on the table, and I will tell you something.'

The man sat down, looking dazed and helpless.

Amy sat by him, still holding his hands.

'I will tell you a story,' she said.

The man listened, with a puzzled stare at Amy's face. Every now and then he sprang up. Then Amy said, 'No, John, I have not done; sit down again.' And the man obeyed.

Somehow people felt they must obey Amy. She spoke so quietly and firmly, and she looked so kind and friendly all the time.

Two hours passed. The man now seemed quiet, and in possession of his senses.

'Can I trust you to go up to bed?' said Amy.

'Yes, Miss.'

'Will you promise me to go up quietly, not to speak a word, and not to do anything to disturb your wife or your children?'

'Yes, Miss.'

'Now remember, you have promised me this, I think I may trust you. I will stay down here till you are safe in bed; then you may call out and I will go upstairs and wish you 'Good night,' and see that you are all right. Be as quick as you can.'

John went up the ladder. By-and-by he called out, 'All right, Miss.'

Amy went up to the bedroom door, and saw that all was quiet. 'Good night, John,' she said; 'go to sleep, and be kind to your wife and children tomorrow morning.'

At this moment two servants arrived. Amy had been missed and the maid had told them where she was. So her strange expedition had been discovered, and she was brought home safely.

I do not think that Amy is to be considered an example for other girls, either in the affair of the poachers, or in that of the tipsy man. But it proved to be well for her in later years that she had accustomed herself to have no fear of rough, wild people. God, who sees the end from the beginning, often allows us, whilst we are still far from him, to learn in all sorts of strange ways the things which will help us later on for the work he means us to do. And one day Amy would have to be with wild people, more dangerous than the poachers or the drunkards she was with in Germany and in England.

Soon after this, Amy came back to her old neighbourhood, though not to the house with oak woods and the ponds of water-lilies. It was to a house near the old one, with a large, beautiful garden. And there, in the shady seats and arbours, she worked hard at her studies.

I then saw her again; she was still full of plans for making drunken people sober, and also for making dirty people clean. This last plan seemed to be her chief thought. If only, she thought, a number of rich people in the neighbourhood would join together, to supply the poorest people with soap and sponges, brushes and combs, baths and towels, a great deal of illness would be prevented, and children would more often grow up strong and healthy. Amy asked me to come on certain days to talk over these plans. She also invited a poor woman, who know how things could be managed in small cottages, and who could tell how much of these great plans it would be at all possible to carry out. I do not think, however, much was done after all, except that Amy gave away great numbers of tracts about health and cleanliness.

I liked to show her that I was willing to help her in these plans for people's bodies; for I thought if I did, I might get her to listen to something about their souls and about her own. Amy did not hide from me that she had no belief in the Bible herself. She did not think it mattered at all what anybody believed. She had been brought up to think that everyone ought to be free to choose what religion they liked best, and that as different people believed different things, it was impossible to find out what was the right belief. Therefore, Amy thought, it is best not to trouble oneself at all about what people believe, but do all one can to make them happy and comfortable. This, she thought, was wise and sensible. We had long talks on these subjects, and it was then that I found out why Amy denied herself and wore very cheap clothes, and went to very few amusements.

'Suppose,' she said, 'I were starving, and had no blankets and no fire, do you think it would be sensible for me, if I got a little money, to spend it in ornaments or lace, or concert tickets? Ought I not to buy coals and food? Now, does it really matter more that I should have coals and food, than that other people should have them? Of course it does not. So now, if I have more money than I want for clothes and food, would it be sensible for me to buy finery, or concert tickets, when other people close by are starving and cold? Ought I not to buy clothes and food for them?'

I could not find fault with Amy's reasoning; but when I began to speak of their souls, and of the great eternity towards which all were travelling, she gave me to understand that she thought people very foolish who troubled themselves about those matters.

'God is very kind,' she said, 'and he is sure to make everyone happy at last.'

85

This seemed to be to her an excuse for forgetting him now, and for living as though he were only a fable. Amy had never known that God must be just as well as kind, and that sin can never be to him a matter of indifference. She reckoned that God thought lightly of sin as men do, even more so. It certainly did not trouble her that she was a sinner.

However, suddenly a great change came in Amy's way of thinking. All at once it seemed to dawn upon her mind that sin is to the soul a far greater evil than dirt is to the body. She had begun to read the Bible, which she found at first to be only a beautiful and interesting book. But the entrance of God's word giveth light - it giveth understanding to the simple. It was from reading the Bible that she began to feel the exceeding sinfulness of sin, and to see that if there is a God who is good and just, he must hate that which is evil.

So now, perhaps, you will think Amy began to care more for the sin of her neighbours than for their dirt and misery. But I think the truth was that when Amy's eyes were opened, it was not the sin of her neighbours but her own sin that filled her with fear and sorrow. She saw that while she had been pitying the drunkards and the selfish, she had been no better than they were in the eyes of God. She had been looking out, like the lawyer in the 10th chapter of Luke, for the neighbour to whom she could do good, and it had never struck her that what she needed was a neighbour who could do good to her. She had not known she was like the man who fell among thieves, who was helpless and penniless. The plain truth of the matter was she needed to be saved from her sins before she could do anything pleasing to God. But how was she to be saved? Would all her work for the poor save her? No. She saw that if a servant has done wrong to his master, no kindness to his fellow-servants will make up for that. It is his master who has to be satisfied about his conduct. Would her prayers save her? Perhaps they might, she thought. But how could she know that they would? And after all, why should God pass over her sin just because she wished him to do so? Would that be justice?

Amy said little about her great unhappiness, but she became more miserable each day. She was now very willing that we should read the Bible together. She seemed to listen for her life, but would seldom make any remark. It was difficult to know what to say to her, as at the time one could not know her thoughts and feelings.

One day she looked more than usually miserable. We had both been taken by a friend for a long drive. Amy, who had formerly been so bright and cheerful, scarcely spoke a word. The next morning I had a letter from her. It had been written in the evening after the drive. She told me that she was now, for the first time in her life, really and perfectly happy. She said that for weeks past she had been without hope and comfort. She had seen her whole past life to be but one great sin, for she had been living without God, and had seen no beauty in Christ that she should desire him. All her plans for the poor and drunkards had only been plans for trying to make them happy and comfortable without God. Each day she had seen more clearly that she was one of the chief of sinners.

'And today,' she said, 'I felt that I could do nothing but tell him how wicked, how hopeless I was, and confess my whole life to him as nothing but sin and foolishness. And then he showed me the door of hope; he showed me that Jesus had borne my sins in his own body on the cross and that they were all gone – gone for ever from the sight of God, and that I am whiter than snow, washed in his blood, and saved for evermore.'

These were, as far as I can remember them, the words of Amy's letter.

Amy's Mission

And now began the second part of Amy's life — or rather, now her life really began — her life as a child of God. We had very pleasant days together after this. Amy would come over early in the morning, and by seven o'clock we were out in the garden under the great mulberry tree with our Bibles. We both agreed to learn Hebrew, that we might read the Psalms and Proverbs more carefully. In the meantime we read the Gospels and the Epistles. Amy said all seemed new to her. The third chapter of John was a great delight to her, especially the verse about the serpent in the wilderness. She told me she had been talking to her brother Richard about this verse. She hoped that he would see that it is nothing that we can do or feel that saves us — only Christ. We are saved because of Christ's great work on the cross. And this work was not done because we loved him, but because we hated him, and he loved us. This great work was done and finished so that now we only have to look up to him and thank him for it, believing that eternal life is given to us as soon as we look to Christ. We are not only given forgiveness, full, free, perfect forgiveness, but we are given the glorious life that is in Christ in heaven, the life that can never end.

You may be quite sure that Amy's whole life was changed after this. She cared now more than ever for the poor and miserable. But it was not only for their bodies that she now cared: she told them of Jesus — Jesus, the Saviour not only from drunkenness, but from all sin and from all misery.

'What a glorious life it is that God gives us!' she said to me. 'We know we are safe for ever, we know that we are going to be with him in heaven, and now, down here, we can please him and do his work.'

She showed me three verses in the Psalms, which gave her great pleasure. First in Psalm 119 verse 3 she read, 'They also do no iniquity: they walk in his ways.' Then, in the same Psalm at verse 32, 'I will run in the way of your commandments, when you shall enlarge my heart.' Then, in Psalm 150 verse 4, 'Praise him with the timbrel and dance.'

'Isn't that beautiful?' she said. 'First we learn to walk in God's ways; then, as we get on, he teaches us to run; and at last, when we get to the end, and there is no further to go, we dance. It is all joy then.'

But these pleasant readings with Amy soon came to an end. Her mother died, and Amy went quite far away to live with some relations. She did not remain there for long, for when they found Amy had no pleasure in their balls and parties, and even refused to go to them, they were glad she should find a home somewhere else. Amy went from one relation to another. Few understood all that God had done for her, and many were displeased with her, or amused at her odd ways, as they thought them.

Thus time went on, and one day I heard that Amy was going to be married to a missionary, and was going to India. I saw her no more for a long while, and heard very little about her. She was not long in India, but afterwards she lived in a part of England far away from her old home. As the years passed by she was very busy with three little girls to teach and take care of. And as she was not rich, she made their clothes, and worked very hard, in addition to all that she had to do out of the house.

She was not very strong, and had for some time to leave England to live in a warmer country. So for a year or more she had a home in the quiet old town of Pisa. While there her little girls liked to see the leaning tower, and to wander about in the beautiful old white marble cloisters, called the Campo Santo. The green space inside these cloisters is said to be made of earth brought in ships from Jerusalem, many hundred years ago. The people who lived there, knew less than you know about the Lord Jesus and his work. But some loved him in a simple way. They liked to think that the green grass, and the wild daffodils, that were so pleasant to look at, grew out of the earth that his feet had walked upon. But it is better to know him as we may know him now, where he is, in heaven.

Amy did not go on long living at Pisa. For a short time she came back to England. But she began to cough, and grew very thin and weak, so the doctors said she must go and live always near the Mediterranean. Several places were thought of. At last it was settled that all the family should go

to Syria and find a home there. They went first to
Beirut, and whilst they were looking for a house,
they lodged with a Mrs Mott, who lived in a house of
her own at Beirut, and had under her care a great
number of schools for Syrian children.

These schools were scattered about over the
mountains of Lebanon, and on the great plain below.
Mohammedan girls, Druse girls, Jewish girls, and
the daughters of the Christians of the Greek Church
all came to these schools. They were all taught the
Bible, as well as other things which are useful for
girls to know. I have had many letters from some of
these girls, and have been glad to hear of some of
them becoming true servants of God, and teaching
the gospel in their turn to other children.

Amy was very glad to help in this work, and it
was agreed that several schools should be put under
her care. She undertook to visit them from time to
time, and looked after both teachers and children.
Of course it was necessary to learn Arabic, though
most of the children were taught French and English
as well. Amy could learn languages very quickly.
Less than three months after they arrived at Beirut,
I had a letter from her. She said 'We are living a sort
of gipsy life in a very odd house. I have only an
Arab servant, so I am obliged to talk as much Arabic
as I can. My husband went to the mountains today
for a few days, and as my servant goes home in
the evening, I and the children are all alone.' The
children were then ten and seven and five years
old. Her husband had gone to the mountains to look
for a house, and discovered one in a little village

called Sook, on the top of the Lebanon. It had formerly been inhabited by American missionaries and was now in rather a ruinous state, neglected and untidy. So much so that if they wanted to hang up anything, the nails would not stick in the walls, they were so damp and mouldy. 'The road up to it,' a friend wrote, 'is most extraordinary; the path is very narrow, with steep steps all the way.'

But Amy was quite contented, and the fine mountain air made her feel strong and well again. She had to spend a good deal of time out of doors, because the schools she had to visit were many miles apart. The only way to get about was on horseback, and for a time the only horse they could get was one that was never content till he had kicked off his rider. But with Amy he was always good and gentle. She was the only person who could groom and harness him, and she felt quite safe on his back riding alone over the lonely mountains and rocky paths. The little girls remember how sometimes she was sent for in the middle of the night. Perhaps someone was ill, or something was needed in a hurry. But by day or by night Amy was ready to go, and the Lord watched over her, and kept her from harm.

The house at Sook was not at all like an English house. It was built round three sides of a square court, which was roofed in. The fourth side stood open, and looked over the flat roof of the house in front, which stood lower down the steep hill side. The little girls had their gardens round the pillars in the court, and they went out to play on the flat housetop. From their playground they had a magnificent view over the great plain, which stretches from the foot of the Lebanon to Beirut, and Tyre and Sidon. Fourteen miles off they could see the blue Mediterranean, with the white sails passing to and fro. At the back of the house was a mulberry garden, which ran up the hillside above. There were large shady plum trees as well. The village down below was inhabited by Greek Christians and Mohammedans, and in summer Europeans came from Beirut to have some mountain air.

A few months after Amy had set up home there, she wrote me a letter. She said: 'I should have written sooner, but I have much to do here. I have only a fifteen-year-old Arab girl as a servant and yet there is much more to be done in the household than in England. For instance, we cannot get wholesome flour for bread, so we buy wheat, which has to be washed and cleaned at home. There is a mill near, where we get it ground, but we have to make the bread. My maid also cleans the barley for the horse, and makes the butter, so I often have to help in many ways.

'Then I have to teach the children. I spend as much time as I can in learning Arabic. I can do little amongst the people till I can speak it more. I can read books pretty well, and also the Bible I can understand tolerably with a dictionary, but I must learn to talk.

A few days ago a Druse sheikh was at our house. I spoke to him of Christ as the only Saviour. He came over from the other side of the room, and sat close to me, trying so earnestly to understand

94

all I was saying to him. I think he is one of the most sincere of the Druses, and one who is almost persuaded to be a Christian, but is kept back by fear of persecution.

'I feel such compassion for the Druses; they are a fine race of men, and though there is much to be said against them, it is unjust to lay on them the whole blame of the massacre of Christians in 1860. The Greeks and Maronites provoked them almost to desperation, and the Mohammedans fanned the flame, hoping to exterminate the Christians by means of the Druses.

'A Druse village near here has begged several times to have Christian school. It seems so hard to refuse such a request, but one cannot do it without money.'

Amy longed for some people to talk to, who really knew the love of Christ. Though the quiet village life was pleasant, she seemed to be far away from any who could understand her thoughts. 'But,' she said, 'the Lord keeps me near to himself, and he will guide me. As to my body, I am quite strong and well, and the children too. They live rather a wild mountain life, but learn to be useful in many ways. I find it very pleasant riding over the mountains. The cassia trees in flower all along the paths are so sweet. In the mountains it is rather cold, but though it is December we have not yet had a fire. The cyclamens are all in flower, and the scarlet and purple anemones. The crocuses are almost over; they were very pretty, purple, white and gold peeping amongst the grey rocks.'

Amy took some time to explain to me a little about the different kinds of people from the Lebanon and all around it. In the village of Sook most of the people called themselves Christians. Some went to a Protestant church. Some belonged to the Greek Church, which is the same as the Roman Catholic in most things, but instead of the Pope they have the Patriarch of Constantinople as the chief bishop. All these people at Sook were Syrians. In some of the villages near by there were Syrian Roman Catholics, and other villages were Mohammedan. Some villages were inhabited by a sect of Roman Catholics called Maronites, who had lived on the mountains of Lebanon for many centuries. But a great many of the villages were inhabited only by Druses.

The Druse religion I cannot explain to you. It seems they were at first a Mohammedan sect. But at present they differ very much from the Mohammedans. If you ask a poor Druse what he believes, he says, 'I believe what the learned believe.' If you ask those who are considered 'learned,' they say their religion is a secret.

It was unfortunate that the Druses gained most of their knowledge of Christianity from the Greek or Roman Catholic churches. What they thought of as Christianity was in fact idolatry. They needed to be shown the real Christ and the truth of God's word.

The Druses had small square buildings on the highest peaks of the mountains. In these places they had their worship; but as Europeans can never go inside these buildings, I can tell you nothing of what was said or done there. Amy felt a great interest in these people though, because the native Christians seemed to consider it almost impossible that a Druse could be converted. Even the Protestants seem to have understood very little of the power and love of God. Amy said of them, 'At all events, one must feel thankful that many of these Protestants are saved, though they do not realise it, and go on praying earnestly for forgiveness.'

How often we ask God to do what he has already done! If we truly believe in Jesus, 'we have our sins forgiven, according to the riches of his grace.' And it is said, 'By him' (Jesus), 'all who believe are' (not shall be) 'justified from all things.'

'Sometimes,' Amy would say, 'I think of all the preaching and teaching you hear in England, and feel as Moses may have felt on the barren Moabite mountains, looking into the land flowing with milk and honey. Yet sometimes, though I long to be with you, I almost feel as if Christ has become more and more precious the more I am cut off from all outer help.'

Then one day Amy paid a visit to a Druse sheikh and when she said that she could read Arabic better than she could speak it, he went to a table in the corner of a room, and brought from it a Bible, the only book in the room, and probably in the house, and asked Amy to read.

'We saw his wife, too,' Amy wrote. 'Poor thing! I longed for her to know the love of Christ. I cannot understand how Christians go on as they do; saved by the blood of Christ, but beyond that seeing nothing more. Oh that we may know more of Jesus!

97

'I have much to be thankful for, though I do long for communion with the Lord's faithful people. Still, the Lord himself is enough to fill our hearts, and perhaps when we feel left alone with him only, we learn most of his love and sympathy. There are, I believe, some true Christians amongst the Arabs here, but I cannot speak Arabic enough yet to have much conversation with them. I have been reading lately with the children the history of David and Solomon, and have been struck with the contrast between David's devotion to the house of the Lord and the coldness of Christians towards the house of the Lord today.'

Amy's letter reminded me of what the house of the Lord really is. Do you know what this means? What is the house of the Lord today? Does it mean a church built of stones and mortar? No. God does not dwell in temples made with hands. Yet God has a house now, down here on the earth. One house only, a house far more precious in his sight than the glorious temple, which Solomon built of gold and silver and precious stones. For God's house now is made of living stone – the chief corner-stone is the Lord Jesus himself, who is called the Stone chosen and precious; and every man, woman and child who believes in Jesus is a stone in this house of God. God himself lives in that house, and fills it with his love. Though his people are scattered far and wide – some English, some Arabs, some Chinese, some in every part of this wide world – yet God sees them all joined together in one by his Holy Spirit;

one great temple where his praise is sung and his blessed name is praised.

Amy went on to tell me how David prepared all that was needed for the Lord's house. Solomon worked diligently to finish it. Yet how much do we love the Lord's people? How much do we love the Lord's house, his church? Christ loved it, and gave himself for it. We must learn to have sympathy with him in his love for it.

Amy felt sad to be separated from God's dear people, and she loved those with whom she could not even talk. She believed they were precious to Christ. Remember this when you meet with any who love the Lord Jesus. It may be some old woman or a little child, or a stranger from another country. If there is anything you can say or do to show your love for those whom the Lord Jesus loves so much, he will remember it one day, however small the little act of love may be.

'This is a wonderful country,' Amy goes on to say. 'At first sight the mountains look dreary and barren, but by-and-by their beauty becomes fascinating, and their wildness makes up for the want of trees and grass. My little girl Edith, from the beginning, has called them the "purple headed mountains", as she mostly sees them at sunset when we go out for a walk.'

Amy's Travels

Little Edith and her sisters had a great pleasure the first year that they spent in Syria. Their father and mother, and a friend who had gone out to Syria to preach the gospel, made a plan for travelling all over the Holy Land. They were to live in tents, which they could easily carry on their horses. Amy knew that the little girls would enjoy this journey, but two of them were still too young to ride on horseback, and there was no other way of travelling. However, their kind mother thought of a plan. She found two large boxes like tea chests, which she fastened together with a long strap. Then they were hung over the back of one of the horses, upon which Amy herself rode. Edith was put into one box, and Persis in the other. May had a horse to herself. They took with them as much food as they could carry, and set off for Jerusalem. There were many places to see on the way to Jerusalem. Some were beautiful, and some had more than beauty to make them worth seeing. There were the places where the Saviour had lived and taught, and worked miracles. Some had changed very little since those wonderful days so long ago. Trees and flowers were there just as they must have been then — the twisted silver-grey olive trees, fig and palm trees, pine trees, and the wild myrtle.

It was in the spring that they travelled so the great scarlet and purple anemones were all out in the olive grounds and fields, and the white cistus, and yellow, prickly broom, and down in the valleys and plains there were fields white and sweet with the little wild narcissus. The girls enjoyed it immensely. Sometimes they complained when there was no food to be had but a little sour bread. But Amy never complained, and was always bright and happy. From Jerusalem they went through the wilderness of Judea, where John preached, and came to the river Jordan, where the banks were covered with willow and oleander, but looked very much the same as when John stood there and saw the heavens opened, and the Holy Spirit descend upon the Son of God. They crossed the Jordan into the land of Bashan, and there they lived for some days in one of the old giant cities, where the great stone houses have been standing empty and deserted for so many ages.

They called them 'giant cities', because so many people have imagined that they were the actual cities built by the race of giants, of whom Og, King of Bashan, was one. 'Probably,' Amy said, 'they are built on the sites of the old cities of the giants, but are not the remains of those cities. Such remains are, perhaps, buried underground. The present cities are by no means gigantic, though certainly very solid, being built entirely of stone. This, however, was simply owing to the scarcity of wood. There are many inscriptions in them, nearly all Greek, a few Arabic, and we saw only one of a character we did not know.'

To one of these old houses Amy invited a great many of the Arabs from the villages nearby. These poor people listened gladly to the word of God, and asked that a school might be opened, that their children might learn to read and hear of Jesus. Up until then Europeans had been afraid to go, because the Arabs had a bad name as robbers and murderers. But to Amy's little party of travellers they were very kind. They brought them food and milk, and they said they were very thankful that Amy had come amongst them to tell them the good news.

The travellers had a pleasant journey back to Sook. The little girls in the boxes had had a fine time of it. They were just as fond of living out-of-doors as their mother had been before them, and children who travel about in comfortable railway carriages, with stuffed cushions, and sleep at grand hotels, and dine at tables, can scarcely imagine how much more amusing these six weeks were spent in the open air, in all sorts of wild and curious places.

Amy had become very fond of the wandering Bedouins during the journey on horseback, when they were so kind and friendly. The whole family wished to go and live beyond the Jordan, at Ramoth Gilead, but they needed a house built there first.

Meanwhile, Amy had made many friends amongst the Mohammedans, and especially amongst the Druses in the villages round Sook. The Druses came in such numbers to the house to hear about the Lord

Jesus, that Amy began to have constant readings with them under the plum trees in the gardens. Some were truly turned to God.

'Oh,' she wrote, 'I long to see Christ himself loved for Himself, not merely truths taught about him! There seems so little warm devotion to him. Still, perhaps, there may be more than we see.'

In the spring of 1872, Amy and her husband and another English preacher, Mr Rose, went for a second time across the Jordan to spend three weeks in Bashan. They took with them a muleteer, who was a Greek Christian, two other muleteers who were Druses; a Maronite lad to look after the horses, and two Mohammedan soldiers. 'All, I was thankful to find,' Amy wrote 'had no fire-arms. The soldiers had swords, but they were used only to cut grass for the horses.'

You must remember that Bashan is not a desert, but a beautiful and fruitful country. At that time it was still much as it was when the three tribes of Reuben, Gad and Manasseh asked Moses to let them stay there. The deep green valleys, filled with willows and oleanders, that grow by the clear mountain streams, are the home of many singing birds. The cuckoo is heard there. The hoopoos, with the golden crests, live in the woods. The fig, and the vine, and the olive grow there in abundance, and in the rich, deep soil everything that is planted flourishes and thrives. We read in the Bible of the oaks of Bashan. One would think at first the country was nothing but a plain, but here and there one comes upon narrow mountain clefts and glens, for the land is a table-land and high above the level of the sea.

'The sheikh of Burak,' Amy wrote, 'received us in a most friendly way. Whilst our supper was cooking, we went to his house. It was one of the old houses where the floor had been freshly made up of stamped clay. His wife brought a large basket tray with bread, butter, dibs (a kind of treacle), and pounded sugar. The sheikh took a piece of bread, dipped it in the butter, then in the dibs, then in the sugar, and ate it before we touched anything, to show, he said, that all was free from poison. We were abundantly supplied with milk and food for the horses, and supper sent for the soldiers. Indeed throughout our whole journey nothing could exceed the kindness and friendliness of the Druses. Our general plan was to start at about nine in the morning, and to ride about seven hours a day, resting for about an hour at noon.

'When we arrived at the village where we meant to encamp, we went to the sheikh's house and asked him to show us the best place for the tent. This was often the village threshing floor, and was always freely given. The sheikh would almost always send a servant with coffee for us, and then would come himself to know what we wanted. Butter, milk and eggs were always to be had in plenty and generally they offered us a lamb. It was very interesting to talk to the men, women and children who gathered in numbers round the tent. At sunset the goats came in from pasture, providing us with milk. Mr Rose or I then cooked the supper. Afterwards the sheikh and some of his family would come and spend the evening with us, or I used to sit outside the tent door by the remains of our charcoal fire, talking to the soldiers and villagers till bedtime.'

How many there must be in these lonely villages who in this way heard of the love of Jesus! We shall know some day in how many hearts the seed of the word took root! Amy goes on:

'Our life was, as you may imagine, very primitive. I did not see a chair or a table for three weeks, but I enjoyed it very much. In almost every village the first question asked was, "Will you not give us a school?" it was sad to see these fine, intelligent, brave men unable to read. They have done what they could for their children, and we found several of the boys able to read and write, and most anxious for books. We gave them the book of Genesis and the Epistle to the Romans bound together, the Gospels and Acts in one volume; also *The Blood of Jesus*, and *Come to Jesus*.

'They were delighted to have these books. In one village the children brought eggs for them. At one town the sheikh said, "The English seem to have forgotten us. We have begged and prayed for teachers, but none come. It seems no use to ask any more." At one village there were twenty or thirty ignorant Christians, very superstitious and dark. They had only one Bible amongst them. My husband preached to them on Sunday morning. In the afternoon there was a meeting, with all of us chatting and sitting on mats on the floor in one of the old stone houses. In one village there were many children who could read, and who were so eager for books we could not satisfy them. We spent Sunday there. I could not leave the tent owing to the number of people continually coming. I sat by the door all the morning talking to them. Another meeting was held in one of the houses, but it was a stormy one. A Maronite priest came in, and was very violent. He wished to stop the meeting. The owner of the house was very wrathful, for he maintained he had a right to hear and read the Bible in his own house, and to ask anyone he liked to come and teach him.

'When we camped amongst the Arabs, they were quite as friendly as the Druses, and gave us plenty of milk and cheese. It seems very desirable that a Christian family should go and live amongst these people. A missionary asked me the other day if I would go. I would most gladly, and my husband is willing to go for a year at least. Will you pray that we may see the Lord's will clearly? Pray also that suitable teachers may be found who would preach the gospel fully.'

Perhaps Amy thought, during these wanderings, of the days so long ago, when she had set her heart on living out-of-doors! How little had she imagined then how she was to have her wish granted! Not in the oak woods of England, but in the wild plain of Bashan. Not to please herself, but as a messenger from the Lord Jesus, to make him known where others had feared to go. When she got back to Sook, she was glad to find that several Syrian Christians were willing to go and open schools in Bashan. She felt sure the Druses would receive them gladly and treat them kindly. So with many prayers these teachers were sent to the distant villages, and they promised to send word from time to time about how they were getting on.

Soon after this Amy's husband went for a time to England, and she was left with the three little girls at Sook. There was now a great deal to do, for there were so many who were longing to hear the gospel, especially amongst the Druses. Amy would go alone, or with one of the little girls, from one Druse village to another, read and talk from house to house, and when she was tired she would ask if she might lie down on the mat, and go to sleep for a little while. Then she would wake up refreshed, eat any of the food they offered her, and go on again.

'I am happy,' she wrote, 'in feeling that the Lord is guiding me, and even though I cannot have the teaching and the Christian fellowship that are so precious to me, I have Christ — Christ in glory! That means everything. God has given me a very active life, and having been here so long, I can often do little things to help people who do not know the language or customs. I can hardly describe the various things I often find I can do to help people. All sorts of things happen which couldn't happen in England and I may be wanted at all sorts of times.

'Only a little while ago a horseman came up for me from Beirut, in the middle of the night; and again, last week, I had to ride down, and come up late at night, only staying there half-an-hour. The horse was a very swift one, so I managed the whole journey in about four and-a-half hours.

'I do seek to do all just simply for the Lord, and I am thankful to him for giving me these things to do, and for keeping me so wonderfully well in health. This climate seems to give me strength for almost anything.

'Can you send me any short tracts that might be translated for the Moslems? Just now many seem to be taught by the word of God, without any human help. Some are almost Christians and confess in a most wonderful way, that Christ is God. It is this that has always been the great difficulty with Moslems. Many confess that he died for us and that he is the only Saviour. They believe that the Bible is the word of God, though they think the Koran is also. Several have been imprisoned for their belief, but they are still Moslems, in name at least, so nothing worse was done to them. I don't think a Moslem who became a Christian would be openly put to death by the government, but he would be persecuted and, perhaps, murdered privately.'

Soon after this a sad time came. For a while the teachers who had been sent to Bashan sent good accounts of their schools, and all seemed well. But one day news came that the best of the teachers, a Syrian, called Girius, had been murdered by the Druses, and another robbed, and beaten, and sent back quite destitute to Damascus.

Amy wrote: 'I felt quite overwhelmed when we heard this. Poor Girius had left his wife and little children in the Lebanon. It was terrible to think of them. What a blow it was to the work. It upset me to think of the wickedness of the Druses, whom I had loved and trusted. When the news came, I was on the roof with a Druse sheikh. He said, "I will not believe it. If Girius has been murdered, it is not by our people." He wanted to get a horse to go at once to Bashan to see if it were true. But it was settled at last that a young Englishman, who was a teacher in the Lebanon schools, should go instead, and that a Syrian doctor should go with him. They went to Beirut first to get an order from the governor for the body of Girius to be given up to them.'

The morning they left, Shibbley, the most powerful of the Lebanon sheikhs, came to see me; he, too, refused to believe that his people had committed such a crime. But I felt very sad, and in the afternoon I took the two youngest girls, and went with another Druse sheikh, called Chatar, to a lonely part of the mountains. We sat there and read the gospel. It comforted me to hear the way in which Chatar talked to me. "Do not let your faith be weak," he said; "God is able to turn this sorrow into joy, or to bring blessings out of it, such as you do not expect, and then you will praise him for the trouble."

'The next day I was surpised to meet one of my teachers from Bashan. You may imagine my joy when he gave me a letter from Girius himself! I didn't stop to read it, for I knew his writing. I went off directly to the Druses. I found Chatar asleep in his house. He looked quite bewildered when I woke him up, but as soon as he understood the matter, his delight was great, and we thanked God together. Sheikh Shibbley was just as pleased. I gave him the letter and he read it to me. Girius, it seems, had been very ill, and was still so, but no one had harmed him, or had any intention of doing so. Sheikh Shibbley and I had a long and interesting conversation. I long so much for this man's conversion. Do pray for him. He is so much more humble than he was, which is hopeful.'

Soon after this, two more teachers came back from Bashan, and said they had been very kindly treated by the Druses, but that Girius was still very ill. He needed someone to go and look after him.

'But,' wrote Amy, 'in spite of all that was told of the Druses, not a Christian would go! I couldn't find one who had sufficient faith in God, or love for his brother, to go to the poor sick teacher in his loneliness; so I asked Chatar to go.

'Alone he set out on a cold morning. When he left our house he said to me, "Pray for me as your brother." He reached Damascus in two days, and Elkurieh, in Bashan, in three days more. He found Girius very ill, but by making a comfortable bed on a camel's back for him, he brought him safely to some relations he has at Damascus. From there Girius wrote to me: "Sheikh Chatar came to me as an angel from heaven." Girius had been very kindly treated in Bashan but was, of course, glad to be nursed by his friends at Damascus and to get the money which we sent by Chatar.'

The sad thing was, that the false report of Girius' murder had been spread by two teachers who had come back to the Lebanon. On their way through Damascus they had invented the story of the murder of Girius. This was, of course, to excuse themselves for leaving their work in Bashan. And these men called themselves Christians! When Chatar came back to the Lebanon, Amy wrote —

'I asked Chatar to tell me exactly how the Druses in Bashan felt towards the Christian teachers. He replied: "The sheikhs all say that they will receive the teachers with all courtesy and friendliness. They wish to have their children taught but they will not have any more Christian teachers. They were unjustly accused of evil. If a Christian teacher comes and dies amongst them they are afraid that they will be accused of murder. They are still quite willing that the Bible, and the Bible alone, should be taught but they only want teachers who are Druses."

'The sheikh of Elkurieh wrote me a letter in which he says, "Could you believe I should make such a bad return for your kindness as to murder your teacher?"

'Now I really do not know where to look for any teachers. Those we did send called themselves Christians and were the best we knew of and yet they have neither faith, nor love, nor courage, nor truth! I am myself inclined to send Druses, and the word of God, and leave the work more fully in God's hands. My own belief is that many of the Druses are more truly Christians than many who have been calling themselves Christians.

'I said to Chatar one day, "How is it that when I talk to Sheikh Shibbley about Christ, he says he cannot believe that he is the Son of God, and yet the Druse boys at the school, when I ask them to say an English sentence, almost always say, 'Jesus Christ is God.' Do their parents know of this, and do they like them to say it?"

'Chatar answered. "Perhaps their parents would not say it themselves, but the truth is finding its way into the hearts of the children. The parents cannot prevent it."

'I told him we were astonished at the boys, because they were mostly new boys, who had had very little teaching. He replied, "What teaching had I before I came to you? Hardly any from men; but the Holy Spirit had taught my heart."

'A few of the Druse women spent the evening here a few days ago. It was very pleasant, and very un-English. We all sat on the ground, and the husband of one of them read aloud to us. Amongst other chapters, he read John chapter 4, and several times he repeated with earnestness the forty-second verse, "And said unto the woman, Now we believe, not because of thy saying: for we have heard him ourselves, and know that this is indeed the Christ, the Saviour of the world." Pray for this people. Oh, pray for them that they may come fully to the Lord, not to the so-called Christianity that they see in others around them.'

Amy knew that there were some Christians who cared for the souls of the Druses. Christians from Europe and America had gone amongst them, both on the Lebanon and in Bashan. The problem seemed to be with the native Christians who looked on the Druses in the same way as the Jews looked on the Samaritains in Bible times. They actually despised them.

'I believe more and more firmly,' Amy went on to say, 'in the work of the Spirit alone, teaching through the word. One thing which has led me to this is the history of a young man, for whom I beg you to pray. He is a Moslem and lives at a village called Raifoon, where he is a schoolmaster. When my husband went to preach at Raifoon, this young man, Sheikh Hassan, opposed him bitterly. However, some time ago, he asked for a Bible. We gave him one, telling him not to throw it away if he did not like it, but to return it to us. This he promised to do. He began to read from the beginning, straight on. One day I met him in a house where I was visiting. I asked him to read for me the account of the Passover. He objected a little, because he said he had not got to that part, and he must read straight on. "But," he added, "I am not going to give up this book." Some time later I went to a shop, and found Sheikh Hassan sitting there. He told me he was still reading the Bible. "You are reading the Bible," I said, "and I have been reading the Koran."

'The shopkeeper said, "It is not a sin to read the Koran."

'"No," I said; "there are some good things in the Koran. Mohammed was right in saying that idols are not to be worshipped."

'"Yes," said Sheikh Hassan, "Mohammed was an instrument against idolatry, but he was a man, as we are. He was no Saviour."

'"True," I said, "Mohammed could save no one. There is but one Saviour, even Jesus Christ."

113

'"Oh," said the shopkeeper, who was a professing Christian, "Sheikh Hassan doesn't believe that!"

'Hassan looked a little grieved. "I have not come to the New Testament yet," he said; "but I know that salvation must come from God alone. Have you got a Bible?"

'The shopkeeper acknowledged he had not. "Then," said Hassan, "I advise you to give up something, even your daily food, to get one."

'So you can understand I feel led more and more to rest on the word alone. The so-called Christians, even those who are perhaps really Christians, are very cold. I have not yet met with one of them who could say he knew he was saved. I would be thankful if there were some earnest man who could teach others. I feel that all I can do is live amongst the people and love them.

'I am quite strong, wonderfully so, as I live entirely on bread and Arabic coffee. I often think of you, and long for such teaching as you get; but pray for me that the Lord himself may teach me. I should so like to see you, but otherwise have no wish to return to England.

'A Bedouin was baptized at our house last Sunday. His confession of Christ as the Son of God and Saviour of the world was quite clear. A Christian here asked him just before he was baptized if he thought being baptized with water would save him. He answered: "Will the medicine heal the sore on the sheep's skin if it be rubbed on the wool?"'

As time went on, one Druse after another began to ask to hear more of the Lord Jesus. Some believed and were saved, and Amy would have been thankful if a Christian preacher could have been found amongst them.

She wrote in the year 1873: 'I am really longing for some preacher of the gospel to come here. It seems so useless for me to be here, and yet I cannot help feeling that the Lord placed me here, and I can only wait for him to use me.'

The Druses came to Amy about all their concerns, knowing that she cared for them. For instance, one day in Beirut, some men from the mountains were bringing in horses for sale. In the narrow streets the horses suddenly began to fight, and became so wild the men fled to a safe distance, and looked on in dismay. At last one said, 'Oh, if only that kind lady were here! She would tell us what to do.'

'She is here,' said one, 'I saw her go down to the market.'

Immediately the men ran off to the market and returned with Amy, who walked quietly amongst the horses and separated them. It was strange to see the little delicate-looking Englishwoman managing the restive horses, whilst their owners, ten strong men, stood at a distance, afraid to go near them.

'However,' Amy wrote, 'I believe I am in my right place and in the meantime the Lord teaches me. The Druses ask me to say to you that they want you to pray for them, and I entreat you to do so. One of them this morning, for the first time, prayed himself. It was very cheering to hear one of these poor despised ones praying in the Name of Jesus. The Syrian Christians speak of them as dogs and swine, to whom the pearls and the holy things are not to be given.'

During this time Amy's little girls thoroughly enjoyed their life on the Lebanon. They learned how to read and talk Arabic, and Amy hoped that they would be able to read the Gospel to some who could not read themselves. Persis was, however, making plans on her own, whilst she was playing with her tortoises, or working in her garden; but I do not know whether she told them to her mother. She was allowed to play about near the house, and sometimes wandered as far as an old monastery of Greek monks, into which no women were allowed to go. Persis, however, was only a small child, so the monks were not afraid of breaking their rule by talking to her.

At last they invited her into their chapel, hoping that she would admire the painted pictures before which they knelt to pray. But Persis knew too much of the Bible to enjoy the sight, and she felt quite sure that if she could only get the monks to listen to texts, and hear all that she had to say, they would learn the truth of Jesus Christ. She therefore paid them constant visits, and was disappointed at last to find that the pictures still hung in their places, and the monks showed no sign of repentance. Poor little Persis had to learn long afterwards that Protestants need to be converted just as much as Greek monks, and the time came when she found out that she too needed to hear the voice of Jesus Christ.

When some of the Druses became Christians, Amy began to gather them at the house for about a quarter-of-an-hour every morning. They then all prayed together. One day some poor Druses came from a distant village to the house of Sheikh Chatar. They told him they had heard something about one called Jesus. They wanted someone to go to their village, and tell them about him

Sheikh Chatar replied: 'If you think you will get any money by that means, or get off some punishment for your crimes, it is no use to come to us, for the gospel is not to make people better off, it is to tell them how God saves us from our sins.'

They said they wanted only to be taught, and nothing more whatever. Next week they came again with the same request; but Sheikh Chatar, though he was interested in them, did not feel inclined to trust himself in their village. So he sent them to Amy and warned her that nobody in that village had ever died a natural death. However, Amy was quite ready to go, so, taking her daughter May as a companion, she set off on horseback for the ride of twenty miles.

'It is such an odd place,' she said; 'a little village half in ruins, on a hill in a sort of basin, surrounded by much higher hills, and between it and the sea is a great mound which shuts out all view, except a tiny bit of the sea at each side of it. The road is so bad, I could hardly believe the horses could get down to it.

'The people in the village are in darkness. They know there is a God, and that they are Druses by name, but beyond that they know nothing. There is no one in the village who can read, except one lad, and he reads very badly. They are thought to be extremely wicked people; but they were quite

117

civil and kind to May and me. They gave us sherbert and coffee, and watered our horses, and wanted to kill some chickens and cook them for us. I read and spoke to them from house to house as simply as I could, and they listened very attentively, saying, "We never heard anything like this, neither we nor our fathers." We stayed with them and I promised them before leaving the next day if the Lord permitted me, I would come back before long.'

However, Amy was anxious to find some Christian man to go there, for she did not think that God means women to be preachers.

So she went to a Syrian Christian who lived at Sook, and asked him to go. She said, 'He surprised me by saying he was not ordained. I still asked him to go, but he replied, "What will Sheikh Shibbley say?" Of course I said, "It does not matter whether Sheikh Shibbley wishes it or not. If we ask everybody's permission we shall never speak of Christ at all." Then he said, "People will laugh at you for going to such a village." I told him that didn't matter either; the people of Sarachmool had asked for someone to go, and they should not be refused. He offered to send one of the teachers in his school to go with me, but I knew this young man and did not think he had any care for the souls of others. So I said, "Why will you not go yourself?" He then said "I will write to England and ask for an evangelist to be sent out. But as to myself," he explained, "I have too much to do. I have to see to a large quantity of wheat I have been buying and it has to be stored away. I will see about it by-and-by."'

Amy asked one and then another but all in vain. Some said the Maronites and Greeks must be converted first. Others said it was no use to go to Druses. The only person who could be thought of who was willing to go, was a converted Druse. 'But,' said a Christian lady, 'the converted Druses don't belong to any particular denomination and that is so awkward.'

All that Amy could do was pray that the Lord would send labourers into his harvest. I cannot tell you what happened to the people of Sarachmool: I should like to know.

It was not long after this that a preacher came. He was an American, who had worked for God for a long time in Egypt, and could speak Arabic easily. You can well believe what a great joy this was to Amy. It was not a grief to him that the converted Druses didn't belong to any particular group. They met together, and heard the word of God, and prayed and praised the Lord, and then with some Syrian Christians they ate the Lord's supper. Amy wrote in November 1873, 'I beg of you, and of all who care for the Lord's work in this land, to pray earnestly and constantly. Never did we need it so much as now. Pray for us. Pray for those who, few in number, are standing up boldly for the Lord, and pray for the poor weak ones who have been so long like sheep without a shepherd. Oh, that more knew the peace and joy of going straight to the Lord, and depending only on him! I am so thankful that we can now meet together and break bread in remembrance of him.'

Amy's Home

Amy's letters went on to ask for a parcel of warm clothing to be sent out. The winter was setting in. The olive harvest had been a bad one, and she feared there would be great poverty and suffering amongst the poor. She ended by saying: 'Our future path is unknown to us. For five months, as far as we can judge, we shall be here, but where we shall be after that we cannot tell. The Lord will guide.'

One more letter came, written in December 1873. Amy discussed the plans to fetch from Alexandria a printing press, so that Bibles and Gospel tracts might be printed at Beirut.

'The Druses,' she said, 'are much on my heart, especially those in the Hauran.' She went on to say how much she hoped that the places still in utter darkness would not be left to a dead Christianity and people who only called themselves Christians.

'The Lord is able to raise up teachers. It is to him that we must look so that the full, pure, simple truth may be preached. It is only then that souls will be gathered to the Lord and added to the church. I have not been able to go to Sarachmool,' she adds, 'since the rain. The road is almost impassable.'

'The last few days it has been fine again, and if we have a little more dry weather, I hope to be able to go. I have been encouraged to hear of an old Druse there, named Hamzeh, who has been one of the most bloodthirsty of his people. A young man from a neighbouring village went and spoke to him of Christ. The old man was moved almost to tears, and exclaimed "Why have you never been to tell me this before?"

'The young man came up to me — a long walk over one of the roughest roads — because he said he felt as if he must come and tell me that Hamzeh had listened to him, or rather, had listened to the Word of God.'

Amy had wondered about where she would be in five months' time, however, when the five months were over, she had left her home at Sook for one where there is no loneliness, and no sorrow, and no sin. She would no longer ride down the rocky path to Sarachmool. For some time she had been growing weaker and thinner, and her bad cough had come back. Her husband took her to Beirut to see the doctor. It was hoped she would recover when the winter was over but Amy did not think so herself. The winter turned out, as she had feared, cold and wet. Sometimes it was difficult to get food and medicine due to the rough paths and bad weather.

She wrote in that last letter of December 1873: 'They say it is warm, but I feel it very cold. There are a great number of white crocuses on the mountains. The purple ones are nearly over, and the golden ones just coming. Do not cease to pray for us.' And after this I heard from her no more.

When Amy was able to get down to Beirut, she went to see the doctor. A Syrian Christian, called Miriam, wrote to me afterwards: 'The last time I saw her was nearly a month before she was taken to her heavenly Father. She had come down to Beirut to show herself to the doctor, for she was very weak. One morning she came to see me and said "I must go to bid my little ones good-bye, before I leave them to go to be with him, where there will be no parting any more." She wished me good-bye, saying, "If I can, I will come to see you but if not, I hope to meet with you in heaven."'

After this, when Amy had gone back to Sook, she grew so weak that she could not leave her room. The paths around the village were blocked with snow. It was not easy to get any supplies sent in. A Syrian friend visited and read to her the first three verses of the third chapter of the First Epistle of John: 'Behold what manner of love the Father hath bestowed upon us, that we should be called the sons of God; therefore the world knoweth us not, because it knew him not. Beloved, now are we the sons of God, and it doth not yet appear what we shall be: but we know that, when he shall appear, we shall be like him; for we shall see him as he is. And every man that hath this hope in him purifieth himself, even as he is pure.' Then Amy asked her friend to pray and he prayed in Arabic before bidding her good-bye.

One evening one of the little girls came in to say that one of the little rabbits had been taken away from its mother, and she said it had better be put back before night. A visiting friend said in fun, 'Do you think its mother would ever miss it?' Amy looked at her for a moment, and then her thoughts went back to Christ and she said —

Lord, thou hast here thy ninety and nine –
Are these not enough for thee?
But the Shepherd made answer
"This of Mine hath wandered away from me;
And though the mountains be bare and steep,
I go to the desert to find my sheep."

One morning she awoke and said she had had a delightful dream. She thought she had been travelling through a great plain, with many coming and going across it; that at last she found herself at the top of a high bank, and a sudden gleam of bright light came and showed her, far below, wide and lovely meadows and green valleys; that just beneath her lay white, sparkling snow, into which she flung herself, for it looked so cool and soft, and she felt herself sinking into it in perfect rest and delight. She said in her dream, 'I know that this is dying,' and she thought she spoke some joyful words, and named the name of Jesus. 'It is a little disappointing,' she said, 'to wake and find I am still here.'

'It is so good of the Lord,' were the words that she said most often during that time. 'I cannot cast my burden on the Lord for I have no burden to cast — he has taken it all. It is all Christ and only Christ.'

Yet she talked of things around her, and was pleased when a neighbour brought her baby to see her; inquired after her horse, and about all that went on in the house. She welcomed everyone with a smile, and seemed to have no pain. She talked a great deal about her children, and joined in singing many hymns. 'Tell my brothers and my sister,' she said to her husband, 'that in the hour of death there is nothing to rest upon but the blood of Christ, which was shed for us. Tell them all that I die in perfect peace — perfect peace through our Lord Jesus Christ. Tell those that you think are not saved that all the things of the world are nothing at all. Tell all that are not sure of their salvation not to leave it to the last, and not be taken up with worldly things. Say that I am passing away very happily. I feel as if I could lay my head on the Lord's shoulder. Don't forget anybody. I can't remember all my old friends now. And oh! All your life preach Christ, and nothing but Christ. I don't mean only the death of Christ, but his resurrection and his coming again, and our oneness with him in the glory.' She gave many messages to her friends, and asked that her horses might be given to Sheikh Chatar, which was done as she desired.

Her friend wrote – 'She joined in the night in singing many hymns. I was dozing beside her, being very tired, but I shall never forget the peculiar sweetness of that singing, those "songs in the night." Next morning, very early, she died.'

It was a sad day for many on the Lebanon when they saw the funeral go down the steep rocky path to Beirut. Miriam wrote afterwards – 'I felt I must write and tell you what she has been to us. What she used to do was more than what people knew about. She had so much courage. Amy used to say "I feel the hand of the Lord is working with me, and it is he who gave me strength to go on with what I began." She used to tell us the Lord opened the way always if we wanted to do his will. There is a passage from St Mark (chapter 16: 3-4) which she read to us once to comfort us; "And they said among themselves, who shall roll away the stone from the door of the sepulchre? And when they looked, they saw that the stone was rolled away; for it was very great." This always makes me think of her strong faith in God.

Before Amy was removed for burial at Beirut, a large crowd of natives, gathered at the house. A Syrian Christian read from 1 Corinthians 15 and 1 Thessalonians 4:13-18. Many spoke of her kindness and love to them. They felt that they had lost a true friend.

So now I have told you the story of Amy, or rather I have told you the first part of that wonderful story of God's love and grace, which is the great true story without an end. It is pleasant and good to hear the little beginnings of the lives that will never end. It is wonderful to see how God's great power is shown in the lives of those who have been made alive in him. And it is good to see how wonderfully happy God can make his children here, even when all seems against them, and they have sorrows and troubles all round. I hope that many who read this will learn how to say, 'I cannot cast my burden on the Lord, for I have none to cast, he has taken it all.' When we know the Lord Jesus Christ, we know what these words mean, and we know, too, what he gives us even here, in exchange for the burden — 'joy unspeakable, and full of glory.'

Other Classic Fiction Titles

Saved at Sea
O. F. Walton

The waves are rising and the ship is on the rocks.
Alick and his grandfather set out in their boat to
save as many lives as they can...
Alick finds out that there is a rock that you can
depend on in life, Jesus Christ will always be there -
an anchor, a fortress, stronger than a lighthouse on
the rocks, stronger even than death!

ISBN: 1-85792-795-8

Little Faith
A little girl learns to trust
O.F. Walton

Faith, persecuted by her grandmother when her
mother dies, finds faith and justice.

ISBN: 1 85792 567X

Christie's Old Organ
A little boy's journey to find a home of his own
O.F. Walton

Christie is a street child. He sets out with Treffy, the Organ Grinder, to find a place of peace.

ISBN: 1 85792 5238

A Peep Behind the Scenes
A little girl's journey of discovery
O.F. Walton

Rosalie is forced from place to place with her brutal father's travelling theatre - if only she could find a real loving relationship?

ISBN: 1 85792 5246

A Basket of Flowers
A young girl's fight against injustice
Christoph von Schmid

Falsely accused of theft, thrown from her home, her father dead — Mary learns to trust God.
Exciting tale with a dramatic twist.

ISBN: 1 85792 5254

Staying faithful - Reaching out!

Christian Focus Publications publishes books for adults and children under its three main imprints: Christian Focus, Mentor and Christian Heritage. Our books reflect that God's word is reliable and Jesus is the way to know him, and live for ever with him.

Our children's publication list includes a Sunday school curriculum that covers pre-school to early teens; puzzle and activity books. We also publish personal and family devotional titles, biographies and inspirational stories that children will love.

If you are looking for quality Bible teaching for children then we have an excellent range of Bible story and age specific theological books.

From pre-school to teenage fiction, we have it covered!

Find us at our web page:
www.christianfocus.com